GRAY GHOST

VAL LEON

Printed Worldwide
First Printing 2023
First Edition 2023

ISBN 979-8-9880761-2-4

GRAY GHOST

ACKOWLEDGEMENTS

I would like to thank those people, family and friends that have been supporting me throughout this journey. Those that have attended the events, bought the books, or just been emotionally supportive, please understand that part of this is dedicated to you.

To my son Nate, love watching you grow and becoming a young man. Go out and chase your dreams and never let anybody stop you from achieving them.

To my youngest VJ, the world is yours. The things you do and say never cease to amaze me. My "Baby Einstein" will make the world his playground.

To the Stewart and Wilson family, I love you all. Just know that your support means the world to me.

CHAPTER 1

DOING TIME

You hear the buzz, followed by the locking mechanism releasing the latch on the door. Next, the sound of the heavy iron entrance door opening could be heard as you stepped into the shadow of the door frame, leaving one world, and entering another. From that particular spot, you could see a series of other heavily secured iron doors built to hold the most dangerous men inside.

These doors weren't built to just keep a man physically inside of the small isolating space. They were built to entrap your mind. The doors being the color gray weren't coincidental. Gray represents strength and longevity. A daily reminder that these doors are stronger than you are. A daily reminder that you will be behind these doors for a long time. The gray doors are built to be here longer than you are.

The color gray represents stone. The strongest, toughest rock on earth is a gray rock called a diabase rock. This gray rock is commonly used here for unpaved roads. This gray rock is used for roads so insignificant that no care is provided to pave them because they lead to dead ends. These gray doors lead to insignificant places and dead ends inside of prison.

The color gray is detached. These doors are a reminder of detachment from everything beyond the door, both physically and mentally. Detached from your family. Detached from your dreams. Detached from the daily things you took for granted, like simply walking down the street breathing fresh air smelling of grass and trees. The gray door was a reminder that your walks now consisted of the smell of recycled air pushing the scent of half-bathed men from one space to another.

The color gray is unemotional, lacking empathy, vision, or hope. It is a reminder that on the other side of these gray doors, nobody cares about you. Nobody cares about your goals or dreams. Nobody cares about your fears or desires. These gray doors are a reminder that you are a nobody here. Before walking through these doors, you're stripped of your name to ensure you're reminded of your hopelessness in prison.

I no longer had a name; I was prisoner number 1032625555.

Initially walking through the door, I was greeted like the thousands who came before me and the thousands who'd come after. You are watched like a hawk analyzing its prey, looking for exploitable vulnerabilities. They are watching every step you take. They watch your head, to see if your head is down, defeated, and vulnerable or up, attentive, and strong.

They look into your eyes. Do your eyes represent fear and submissiveness? You learn to always look forward, and never stare at anybody. Never look away too fast when making eye contact, because it signifies weakness. And never look too long because it signifies aggression. The eyes are the key to the soul. As they look into your eyes, they can see if you are the hunter or the prey.

Walking in, I could hear inmates rattling the steel gray bars. I could hear indistinguishable chatter meant to intimidate or generate a reaction. I blocked out the chatter and attempted intimidation, seeming unphased by it all. Though this was my first time in prison, it wasn't my first crime. This was the first time I was caught.

The guard led me to my cell, where an inmate was already there, lying down and reading a book. He barely looked up as they opened the cell to usher me in. The first thing that caught my eye when I walked in was the dirty gray toilet and sink combination on the wall facing the door. The toilet looked as if it had endured a hundred years of fecal matter with an attached sink looking as if it was along for the journey.

A small rectangular cloudy window hung on the wall above the toilet. It was big enough to remind you of all the things you're missing outside; yet, too small to actually see or enjoy any of those things.

I dropped my belongings on the floor as the sound of the clanging gray metal heavy doors shut behind me.

"The top bunk is yours." He finally said, not looking up from his book. "I want to make sure we have an understanding. Don't bring no drugs or trouble into this cell," he stated, still not looking up. "I'm just here to do my time in peace and make it back home to my family" he said, finally looking up.

"I am Derek Stewart. Everybody just calls me Stew." I said as he looked uninterested in learning my name. I placed my clothes in the cubicles attached to the wall which would serve as my closet space for the next 20 years. Throwing my other things on the top bunk, I climbed up to lie down and rest my mind for a while.

As I lay down, he spoke again. "Stew, I'm Mark Wilson. You never responded when I said no drugs nor trouble" he said, awaiting my response.

Leaning over my bunk, I looked down at him as he looked up.

"Mark, I don't do drugs nor drink alcohol, so you won't have to worry about drugs in this cell. As far as that other thing, I'm not here looking for any trouble." I said before lying back down.

"So, Stew, you don't drink nor do drugs? How the hell you end up in here? That is a rhetorical question. So, I don't want to hear your answer."

Standing up, Mark turned to look at me. He continued by telling me of his past addictions; therefore, he doesn't use drugs or drink alcohol. This revelation from Mark started the conversation between us.

"Where you from Stew? I grew up in Albany," he asked.

"I am from Decatur. Been in Dekalb County all my life." I said, proud to represent the east side of Atlanta.

We struck up a good conversation after I got his attention away from the book. We realized that we had a lot of things in common. Mainly a shared hatred for predators and people who took advantage of others just because they could.

"Stew, in here you won't be able to save them all. Better off just minding your business and staying out of the way," he said.

"I don't have a problem minding my business," I told Mark as I started opening up to him. "I just have these dual conflicting personality traits inside of me. I am a criminal and I accept that is who I am. I steal to survive. But it is the other side of me that got me here." I said being interrupted by the sound of those clanging metal locks.

"Time to go eat," Mark announced.

Jumping off my bunk, I headed out the cell with Mark. As we walked, Mark gave me the lay of the land; pointing out who was who in the jail. Jail is very territorial. You need to know the territories and their unwritten rules.

During our walk, it was apparent that Mark had a level of respect in the jail. Most people get to jail and clique up for safety. Mark seemed to walk alone, and you could sense the cliques didn't bother him. Since I was walking with him, I didn't receive the same verbal and nonverbal test from earlier.

Picking up our plates, I looked down as the cafeteria-working inmates slapped measly food portions on my plate. I looked at them with the realization that this what my meals would consist of for the next twenty years.

Mark and I continued to talk as we ate alone at our table. We really seemed to be creating a bond.

He told me about his younger years as a drug addict, including the things he did to feed his drug habit. Mark also told me of his last night as an addict. He shared his experience with the pain of what drugs and alcohol can do to others.

He admitted seeing his loved ones crying, was his breaking point when he decided to kick the drugs and alcohol forever. He had been drug and alcohol-free for three years before his past life as a drug addict caught up with him.

"When you high off that pipe. Nothing else in the world matters. The only thing you think about is what it takes to get that next high, You would do anything to chase it." he said while we sat. "I broke into a house to steal a TV so I could chase that high." he said, recapping the night that landed him here.

"I didn't think anybody would be home so it was going to be an easy score." You could see he was starting to get emotional. "But they were home. The dad startled me when he came into the room with a gun. I had a knife in my hand. I could see the fear in the dad's eyes as he told me to freeze."

You could see Mark's eyes getting glassy at this point.

"I raised the knife toward him. He closed his eyes and pulled the trigger," he said as I listened and thought he must have gotten shot and almost died. As a result of his near death, he decided to kick the drug habit.

"He missed. His little five-year-old daughter came out of her room to investigate the noise. The bullet hit her right in the forehead. " He stated. "I turned to see my worst nightmare as that little girl lie dead on the floor behind me in her own blood."

I was now starting to get emotional.

Mark said, "I dropped the knife and ran out of the door. I never did drugs again in my life. The sight of that little girl haunts me every day."

He told me he checked into a facility the next morning, eventually becoming clean, and changed his life. Mark admitted to getting clean before he got a job at a youth home to pour his life into molding kids.

"Then one morning there was a knock on the door. It was the police. When I looked out the window, I knew what they were here for." he said as he replayed the moment in his mind.

"Are you Mark Wilson? The officer said, when I opened the door."

"Let me just grab my jacket, officer," Mark said without anything further being said. After he'd thought he'd outrun the crack demons and gotten his life together, they showed up years later.

He had really opened up to me, a stranger who he had just met. But it seemed like we had that kind of chemistry from the start. We continued to sit and eat as I observed the multitude of activities going on in the lunchroom.

A man sat at the table next to us eating alone. He was a small guy who looked out of place in here. He looked as if he should be sitting in the church choir; not the penitentiary. He couldn't have been more than 5 feet 6, wearing nerdy-rimmed glasses. I just observed as he sat alone.

Then a group of guys invaded his table. I watched as one took the fruit off his plate, taking a bite out of it.

"What you got for us today, choir boy?" one of them said to him. He looked too scared to answer.

"You ain't got nothing for us today?" another one said as if they already knew the answer. Then he slapped the guy in the head, and they all laughed. A third guy took his food tray. When the little man tried to stand up, one of the guys punched him; knocking him and his glasses to the ground.

Having seen enough, I stood up. Mark grabbed me by the arm. "Remember I said don't bring no trouble to my cell." he reminded me.

The guys saw I had been watching, then standing up.

"You got a problem, homie?" one of them said to me. All three turned their attention from this poor little guy toward me. They approached as I stood there with Mark holding my arm.

I had no intention of causing problems on my first day, but I hate seeing bullies picking on those who can't defend themselves. I pulled my arm away from Mark as the three guys approached me. I stood staring at the apparent ringleader, refusing to flinch. I could feel my jaws tighten as the anger slowly overcame me as a result of what they had done, and now trying to punk me off.

As I previously stated, "the eyes are the key to the soul and they tell it all." I looked this guy eye to eye. It became a battle of the wills to see who would flinch first, as he took another step towards me. He could see the rage in my eyes and at that point he could also see the life leaving.

My stare had become blank, void of emotions and humanity. We were standing face-to-face as everybody watched. His sidekicks stood off to the side as if they were waiting for the action to jump off. I refused to flinch. With the smoldering rage blazing in my eyes, I was ready to take this guy's head off.

He could see it too. "Yeah, I didn't think you had a problem." he said, taking a step back. Sensing he didn't want to have this battle today, but not showing outward signs of backing down. He turned and started walking away. As he walked away, he took the food tray and flipped it on the poor little guy they had been harassing.

The guy picked up his tray and looked at it with the realization all his food had been either taken or spilled on the floor.

"Hey," I said to him, and he turned to look. I tossed him the orange off my plate which I hadn't eaten yet.

"Thank you." The little guy responded. "What do I owe you?" he said.

"Nothing. Don't worry about it." I said, turning my attention away from him and back to my plate.

"I told you not to bring any trouble to my cell. You're about to start a whole damn brawl." Mark said.

I had calmed down by this time and sat down again. "I am not looking to cause any trouble. The question is, were you going to let those three guys jump me?" I said in a sarcastic tone.

He looked at me and said, "the better question is, was defending that guy you don't know worth having those three guys jump you?"

I looked at him and turned to look at this little out-of-place guy again. "I don't know what he did to get here, but that guy doesn't belong here and I am sure he doesn't bother anybody. So, to answer your question, yeah I would have taken on all three of them to defend an innocent person who couldn't defend themselves." I said, grabbing my drink to take a sip.

"If that's your answer and your reason, then I guess I wouldn't have let them jump you. But, do me a favor and don't put me in that position again," Mark said as we changed the subject and continued our meal.

We continued talking. The one thing I took from that little incident was the belief Mark would have my back. He continued to inform me about the prisoners, gangs, guards, and everything else I needed to know.

Then Mark turned to me and said, "Stew, back at the lunch table I saw a guy with some deep-rooted issues come out of you." He continued, "the prison has a new program with a counselor who just lets us talk privately about personal issues and get things off our chest. I have to go in the morning. I think you should go so you can meet Dr. Owens and figure out some of that deep-rooted anger I saw."

I am thinking to myself, did he ask me to go see a psychiatrist? But, really what is wrong with that? I do feel like I lose control sometimes. What triggers me when I see people getting bullied and abused?

"Mark, that does not sound like a bad thing. I may try it." I answered.

I laid down as the lights went out in the housing pod. I lay awake looking at the ceiling and these cylinder block walls with the realization this is what I would call home for the next 20 years.

The next morning, I went with Mark to the therapy session as I told him I would. He told me she was there to do group sessions one day a week and then you could do one day a week of private sessions. This morning was the group session.

I walked in and saw there were about ten other inmates in there. I guess I expected more people since we were in a prison with 1600 inmates who all were here because they were messed up in the mind enough to commit a felony that landed them here.

Since I was new, she introduced herself at the start of the session. She then told me I would have to introduce myself to the group and tell them why I was here. I know I had opened up to Mark, but that was a one-on-one situation with a guy who gained my trust. I was not so sure about opening up in a room full of strangers.

"My name is Stew, and uh. Uh, I don't know why I am here. Mark invited me and I figured it would be a good idea." I said trying to avoid any deep response in this group.

"Well, welcome Stew. Before we are all done, we hope you can figure out why you are here and what you can take from it."

The group session went by pretty fast, but I enjoyed it. Even though I didn't participate much, I felt like I learned a lot by listening. I felt good when it ended.

As we were getting up and walking out, I stopped. "Dr. Owens, Mark mentioned private sessions. How do we go about getting signed up for those?" She smiled as I am sure she felt she had gotten through to me.

"Here. Just fill out this form and pick a day and time," she said, putting a clipboard down on the table.

As Mark and I walked out, he asked what I thought about the session. Even though I had previously opened up to him, that meeting had me feeling a little mentally vulnerable.

"It was alright," I said, downplaying it.

"Alright." he said kind of shocked. "It must have been more than alright. You asked her for a private session." he reminded.

"Man, leave me alone." I joked as we approached the food line.

Everything about jail would be routine. You did the same thing each day. You sat in the same spot each day; therefore, for lunch, we sat at the same table. We are sitting there eating and sure enough this little guy comes to sit alone at the table next to us.

I was feeling a little different after the session, so I thought about asking him to come sit with us. Just as I was thinking about asking him, I saw those same three guys approaching him again.

"What up church boy? What you got for us today?" they said, taking over his table again. This time they sat down and immediately knocked his tray off the table. The same ringleader guy slapped him in the back of his head. He hit him so hard, his forehead bounced off the table.

I could feel the rage overtaking me again. I could feel the grip on my fork tightening as I broke the plastic utensil into pieces in my hand.

As his head hit the table, he rose looking in my direction. Our eyes made contact and I saw the fear in his eyes. I could see the plea for help and his spirit being broken.

Mark grabbed my arm. "Don't bring any trouble to me," he said.

At this point, it was too late. I grabbed my tray with both hands, smashing it into the guy's head. The blow knocked his head into the table knocking him out cold. One of his friends jumped out of his seat, took a wild swing at me.

I ducked and punched him in his gut. He doubled over. I saw the other guy coming around the table to join in. A voice said, "Don't do it," stopping him in his tracks.

As the guy bent over holding his ribs, I bashed him on the side of his head with the tray, knocking him down. Now there was a commotion in the cafeteria as everybody watched and cheered. With one guy laid out cold, I walked over to the other guy and rolled him over; ready to knock his lights out. Climbing on top of him, I reached back to punch him.

"Stew, I think they got the point." I heard Mark say.

I looked at the guy, thinking Mark was probably right. I took my hand and mushed him in the face.

I got up, walked back over to my table, and realized I had just wasted my entire lunch.

The guy on the floor got up, he and the other one grabbed the dude I had knocked unconscious, and they started walking away.

The little guy gathered up his things and walked over to the table.

"Thank you again, you didn't have to do that," he said to me. I told him to not worry, and just go see if he can get some more food. As he turned to walk away, I said to him "tomorrow, why don't you just come sit at our table."

Mark just looked at me and shook his head.

As I sat there, I realized I had nothing left to eat, Mark said "How many times I got to say don't bring any trouble around here." I just looked at him.

"But, I thought you said you wouldn't let them jump me and you would help," I said to him.

"Did the other guy jump in?" he said to me, and I nodded. "Well, I helped as much as I needed, but you need to go see Dr. Owens every day man. You can't try and fight everybody" Mark told me.

"I do not fight anybody; I just defend others," I told him.

"From where I am sitting, it looks like you were fighting to me," Mark said.

I had signed up to see Dr. Owens for a one-on-one session the next day. She heard about my incident in the cafeteria and wanted to focus on that incident.

"Why, tell me in your words what made you want to do that?" she said to me.

I went on to tell her that I feel an attachment to the vulnerable as if I was put here to help them. We spent the entire session with her trying to peel back the layers to understand why I had such an affinity for vulnerable people. Why those situations made me feel the type of rage that I would feel when I saw them.

"Dr. Owens is something wrong with me?" I said to her as I was beginning to doubt myself.

"You are a person of extreme compassion for humanity, nothing is wrong with you. You just need to figure out a way to channel that compassion" she responded.

That first private session with her opened a lot of emotions for me, but I felt it started to explain a lot. After that, I made sure I never missed a group session or my weekly private session with her. Between Dr. Owens and Mark, I had drawn closer to those two people emotionally than I ever had with anybody in life. I felt I could talk to either of them about anything, and they would listen and not judge me.

Over the next few months, I spent more days in solitary that I would have liked to. The situation in the cafeteria wasn't an isolated incident. It became something where I found myself in one incident after another defending somebody in prison.

The lunch area started looking different as that little guy wasn't sitting alone anymore. He was joined by two other guys, who also seemed like they were having a tough time surviving prison. It was as if I had garnered a reputation as a protector, so vulnerable inmates seemed to always spend their free time in my vicinity.

Then the day came that Robert Foster entered our prison doors. I really think he was put in this prison, in this block on purpose. Foster was a convicted serial child murderer and molester. He was convicted of kidnapping, molesting, and killing five kids between the ages of six and ten.

I know they put this man in here to test me. The day he came in, Mark grabbed me, "Whatever you are thinking about today, don't do it." He knew that if I saw this guy in person, I would probably lose it.

And sure enough, I am sitting there eating and he walks by. He sits down alone about three tables away from me. The moment he sat down, the people at the nearby tables all got up and left. Everybody knew me by this time, and they all knew the sight of this guy was probably going to send me over the edge.

I couldn't eat as I sat there staring at him sitting three tables over. "No Stew, don't do it," I heard Mark say. The anger had consumed me again and you could see it in my eyes.

I put my fork down and stood up. I could hear Mark say "Dammit" as he knew what was about to happen, but he was not going to try and stop me.

I walked over and pulled Robert up out of his seat by his neck.

"A six-year-old you piece of shit," I said to him as I unleashed a right hand knocking his tooth out and on the floor.

"You like to touch little kids," I said as I punched him again, and again. Nobody was going to come and stop me as he was the lowest form of criminal in this place.

I put my hands around his neck and took his head and slammed it against the concrete floor.

"You piece of shit!" I screamed as I slammed his head against the floor again. Everybody knew how upset I would get watching grown men being bullied, they could only imagine the rage I would have against a child predator.

I slammed his head against the floor again, and again, and again until I saw the life go out of his eyes. He stopped moving as blood and tissue were plastered all over the floor. The guards came rushing in with riot gear and slammed me face down on the floor.

As they had their knee in my back handcuffing me, I could see Robert's lifeless face.

The guards picked me up by my arms and walked me out of the cafeteria. I was about to be facing a long time in isolation for this one.

As I was being led out, I yelled "I will always protect those that can't protect themselves"

CHAPTER 2

MAKING OF A GHOST

Every person is a product of their environment. Your very being is a product of the things you learned as a kid. The things you saw, the things you were taught, and the values instilled in you. Many like to tell of the fantasy about how somebody escaped the hood and went on to become this great person. That is true in fairy tales and movies, but in real life, you don't ever escape the hood.

You may at some point make enough money to move out of the hood physically, but your mind never escapes the hood. Your mind can't unsee the things you saw, unlearn the things you learned, or change the experiences you had. You carry them with you all the days of your life.

The only difference is the ability of each person to compartmentalize those things. Do you guide your life using those things as learning experiences? Or do those learning experiences guide your life? You see, the former are people that go on to have meaningful lives and become productive citizens. The latter, are the ones that are screwed up in the head and never leave the hood physically or emotionally.

And then you have me. I was the one that was able to guide my life using those things as learning experiences. Except, the only problem, those doors to certain compartments in my mind, they seemed to be too easily stimulated, triggering things with thoughts from the past.

I was born into a world with teenage parents in the hood. Lindsay Stewart was a cute little girl with a promising future. Growing up on the east side of Dekalb County she stood out like a sore thumb. She was smaller than most kids her age. She was a bookworm who enjoyed things other kids in her neighborhood didn't. She was loved by her teachers and was always the top student in her class, no matter the class.

At the age of three, she taught herself how to speak Spanish by simply watching television. By the time she was in kindergarten, she was reading in classes with third graders. She was a person who if born in the lavish neighborhoods of Buckhead, would have been destined to be a CEO or President of the United States. But she was born and raised on the dirty streets of Candler Road in Dekalb County. Being smart and ambitious wasn't always enough to escape these streets.

When she was in the first grade, the most important thing she was learning at school every day was survival.

"Look at her, she thinks she is better than everybody else. Teacher's pet" she heard as she was entering the cafeteria. That comment was a no-win situation in the hood. If you ignored them and kept walking, they feel disrespected as if you don't even respect them enough to challenge them.

If you turned and said something back, that was inviting them to become more aggressive and likely physical. That was the mind of a bully picking on somebody that couldn't fight back. But, Mom was a very small kid, so she chose to ignore them in hopes she could walk away and wouldn't be pursued.

Then suddenly, she was hit in the back of the head with a milk carton. It knocked her down and milk went all over her head and clothes. She lay on the floor for a second and could feel the milk running down her face. She could hear kids giggling and running away.

A teacher saw her on the ground and came over to help her up.

"What happened Lindsay?" she said to her.

Mom just looked at her as tears formed. What was the point of even telling her what had happened? Something like this happened almost every day, and nothing was ever done. All the kids would pretend they did not know who did it. All of the teachers would say there was nothing they co. do if you didn't see who did it. And everybody went about their day like nothing happened except this little six-year-old girl that had nowhere to turn to protect her from the bullies.

Day after day, week after week, it was the same thing. Somebody picking on her just for being different. When you grow up in the hood, teachers and administrators didn't care enough to try and address the bullying, most of them just wanted to get a check and get the hell away from all these bad kids.

But nobody was paying attention to the mental damage these things were doing to a little girl. Nobody was questioning how these things would affect her psyche long term. What kind of permanent damage it was doing to her? She was an elementary school kid and the most important thing to her every day was just to make it back home without getting beat up or having her things taken from her.

Then you had Keith Simmons, my dad. All the struggles my mom had in life with bullies, my dad had it worse because he was a boy. At least most of the girls just taunted most of the time, the boys wanted to always get physical.

That is what drew my mom and dad together at an early age. They both were social outcasts going through the same problems in school with nobody to turn to for help but each other.

Dad was not an extremely small kid like my mom. He was quite the opposite. He was a very tall, skinny goofy kid.

He made decent grades, but he did not like the same things other boys in the hood liked. He was very uncoordinated and could barely walk straight, much less play any sports.

He was allergic to grass, so he was never outside playing with the other kids. He was born with severe astigmatism that caused him to wear very thick glasses at an early age. So here was Dad, this tall, skinny knock-kneed dude with thick glasses.

He tried to blend in the only way most kids in the hood knew, through sports.

He saw kids his age playing basketball at the playground near his house. He decided this would be the day he would test his skills. How hard could it be, he was taller than all of them out there. With his size, of course, somebody was quick to pick him up on their team. He was excited because when they picked teams, he was one of the first ones picked. He had never been anybody's first or favorite, so that made him feel good.

He had watched enough basketball to at least know what to do. The game started, and he ran down near the basket on offense. He threw his hand up asking for the ball with his back to the basket. The kid with the ball whipped a pass into him and this was his chance.

But life is not about fairy tales and perfect endings, he was still this goofy kid with bad eyesight. He saw the ball coming toward him. His eyes got big as he prepared to catch the ball. He reached for the ball and missed it. The ball was coming fast at him, right at his head. He missed the pass and the ball hit him in the face. Knocked him on his back and knocked his glasses off.

He lay on the ground as the other kids were bursting out in laughter. His first chance and it was awful. He got up and went down on defense. He was guarding his man as he received the ball. He had his hands up like he had seen on TV before. The guy catches the ball and takes off dribbling. Dad tried to defend him when he moved, but he was still this goofy kid. He took two steps and then tripped over his own feet and his guy had an easy path to the basket for a layup.

The first time, everybody laughed because it was funny. This time his teammates did not think it was so funny anymore. They take this game seriously, so being a liability on the team was not a fun spot to be in.

The game went on and it was all tied up. Dad had made enough mistakes that nobody would dare throw him the ball, and he figured out it was best, he just tried to stay out of the way on offense and play defense the best he could.

One of his teammates was driving to the basket for what would be a game-winning layup. He was wide open. All my dad had to do was get out of his way. He backed up trying to get out of the way, tripped, and fell to the ground. His teammate was coming hard with the ball and tripped over my dad losing the ball.

A kid from the other team grabbed the loose ball and threw it down court to one of his teammates who made an easy layup to win the game.

"Man, get your sorry ass off the court. You cost us the game" a frustrated little boy said to my dad.

"I am sorry," my dad said to him.

"You are right about that, you are sorry." the boy said as he threw the ball at my dad hitting him in the face. "Get your sorry ass out of here," he said as my dad was reaching to pick up his glasses from being hit by the kid with the ball.

This was life for my mom and dad every day. This is what drew them to one another. Only they could relate to each other about the things they were experiencing. They did not have anybody else to turn to, but at least they could console each other as only a kid in their situation would understand.

This childhood friendship of necessity turned into a teenage relationship. They spent most of their time together as teens because they had no other friends. Bullying in elementary school was bad, but the bullying in middle school was the worst.

They both would skip school together some days, just to get a mental break from the constant bullying. One day skipping school, this childhood friendship that evolved into an innocent teenage relationship went to the next level.

As they were consoling one another, they kissed for the first time. They had both just turned fourteen and were in the eighth grade when they got their first kiss. That kiss led to heavy kissing and the next thing you know; they were both naked at my Grandmom's house.

That was the day I was conceived to two fourteen-year-old sheltered kids that had been the target of bullying all their life.

When I was born, that did not change much about the bullying in my mom's life. Now she just added the pressures of being a teen parent with those of being a constant victim of bullying. The pressure was more than she could take.

When I was three, I came home from getting ice cream with my Grandmom. I was so excited and ran into my mom's room to share some of my ice cream with her. At three years old I opened the door only to see my mom with an extension cord around her neck and the other end tied onto the top bunk bed.

I dropped my ice cream at the door and screamed. My grandmother ran in. When she saw Mom, she immediately grabbed me, covered my eyes, and told me to run to my room. Though I was only three, I was old enough to know what I had just seen.

I was sitting on the floor in my room and hearing my grandmother cry. She never stopped crying, even when the police got there. My mom had left a note. As I sat on the floor, I could hear the police officer read the note in the next room.

"All my life I have been picked on, and there was nobody there to help me. Nobody there for me to turn to, nobody there that cared" I heard him read. Those words would go on to haunt me, as I could never get them out of my head.

People do not understand the long-term mental damage for a three-year-old to find his mother dead. At her funeral, I remember I did not cry. Many thought I may have been too young to understand what was going on, but I was not.

As they were closing the casket, I ran up to my mom one last time. "I'll be there to help you" were my last words as they rolled the casket out of the church.

My dad graduated and got a job. I moved in with him after graduation. The thing is, he was a kid that was bullied, and he grew up. He grew up only to become an adult that was bullied and taken advantage of. My dad did not have much in life, but I knew more than anything in the world, he loved and would protect me. Guess he did not want me to have to go through the things he did as a kid.

I was seven when my dad and I were at the bus stop leaving the mall. He was proud because that day he had bought us some matching Jordans we were going to wear to the circus that weekend. As we sat there waiting on the bus a couple of teenage kids walked by.

"What's in the bag?" one of them said to my dad. I just looked at him wondering what he was going to do. He just picked the bag up and held it with two hands.

"Let me see what is in the bag," the guy repeated.

"That's ok," my dad said to him.

"I didn't ask," the guy said as he snatched the bag from my dad.

My dad had never been one to fight or stand up for himself, but I told you I knew that he would do anything in the world for me. Those were shoes I had wanted for a long time and he finally was able to get them for both of us.

When I saw them take the shoes, I knew they were not giving them back. My dad looked at me and saw a tear forming in my eye. This was going to be the one time he was going to stand up and fight back for himself.

He stood up and reached for the bag. The guy pushed him away. He reached again and the guy swung at him and missed. My dad swung back and hit the guy in his face, and he dropped the bag. My dad picked up the bag and came and sat back down next to me.

"That bag is mine," the guy said as he walked back to my dad sitting down. This time he had a gun extended, pointing it at my dad.

"Should have just given me the bag" he said before he squeezed the trigger. I remember looking over and seeing my dad laying on the ground with his eyes open and a bullet hole in his forehead. I looked up and saw the three guys running off with the bag and my dad, dead on the ground.

I looked at my dad, and tears started flowing. I grabbed his hand, "I am sorry. I told Mom I would be there to help." I am not sure what haunted me the most that day. Seeing my dad get killed or knowing I told my mom I would be there to help, and I did nothing to help.

I was a seven-year-old kid and had witnessed the death of my mom and dad both because of people picking on innocent people just because they felt like they were bigger or badder. That was more death I had seen as a seven-year-old than most Americans ever see in their life.

I did not talk much after my dad was shot. We were poor and had truly little resources, so it was not like my grandmom was going to take me to a therapist to try and process all this death I had witnessed as a little kid.

I would just sit in my room and stare at the wall. Adults did not really know what to do, they would talk to me, and I would just stare at them. I had suppressed the thoughts of seeing my parents dead, I compartmentalized them. But, when I put them away mentally, I put part of my humanity in there with them.

I would rarely go to school. The teachers did not know how to get through to me because I never opened my mouth. I would sit in class and not say a word. Other kids did not bother me though, it was like everybody thought I was crazy and could blow up at any time.

I was eleven when I was at the bus stop. I did not have any friends, and I did not talk to anybody. I was standing there waiting on the school bus. There was a little kid that I saw there every day. I did not know his name and we never spoke. We just were at the same bus stop and rode the bus together each day.

He was standing there with his lunch in a brown paper bag.

"What's in the bag shorty?" I heard a teenage kid ask that little boy. Those words unlocked a compartment in my soul that I had been suppressing. Those words triggered me, and I clenched my fist.

"That looks like my lunch," he said to the little boy as he took the bag from him. Suddenly, I saw flashbacks of my dad laying on the concrete at the bus stop with a bullet in his head and those three guys running away with his bag.

Without thinking, I turned and punched this guy right in the side of his head. He dropped to the ground like a bag of rocks. I jumped on top of him and continued to unleash punch after punch. You could see the blood flying from his mouth as I hit him. Again, and again. The rage had overtaken me.

"Stop picking on people!" I yelled as I punched him. I kept punching until I was too tired to punch anymore. Then I got up and grabbed the kid's lunch and gave it back to him. The kid took the bag and looked at me. Then he looked at this bully lying on the ground, and he smiled and went and sat down to wait on the bus. I walked home and told my grandmom I missed the bus and asked her to take me to school.

At school that day I was called into the principal's office. When I walked in the door, the first thing I saw was that same kid with bandages on his face and two swollen and black eyes. He was sitting next to a lady that looked pissed off.

"Is this the bad-ass kid who jumped my baby?" she said aloud to nobody in particular.

My first thought was, '*I didn't jump on your baby, and did he tell you what he did.*' She went on cursing and yelling at me until the principal came into the waiting room to intervene.

We walked into the principal's office and I immediately asked him "Is my grandma coming?" I was not a disrespectful kid and was not going to feel comfortable arguing with an adult who obviously did not get the whole story.

"We have not been able to get in touch with your grandmother yet," the principal responded.

"So, somebody wants to tell me what happened," the boy's mother said.

The other kid spoke up quick "I told you I didn't want to come in here and nothing happened," he said.

"Something happened boy. Look at your damn face," she said as I just sat there.

"Look, this boy obviously jumped on my son for no reason," she said to the principal, pointing to me.

I still did not speak as the principal asked him "Is that true?"

I was shocked at his response as I knew I was about to get in trouble.

He said, "I didn't tell her it was him." The principal went on and asked his mom why she said it was me who did it. She said some other kids told her they "thought" I was the one.

The principal caught that word, and repeated "they thought" and then he asked the kid again. He repeated that he never told anybody that I jumped on him.

The principal looked at me and told me I could leave. I got up to leave and still had not said anything. As I was walking out the door, I figured I better say something, at least so he could hear it.

"Mr. Jeffries, I would never pick on anybody, and I hate bullies," I said as I looked at him. "People that pick on others for no reason deserve whatever they get," and then I turned to him. "Your son been bullying people forever, and I guess somebody just fought back," I said to the mother as I walked out the door.

That day I felt different. It was not a feeling of joy that I won a fight, or that I beat up a kid. It was a feeling that I kept my word to my mom. I was there to help somebody, even if I was not there to help my mom and dad.

The word about the fight had gotten around the school, and I could see people looking at me differently as I walked the halls. Nobody said anything to me, but you could hear whispers and tell people were watching and talking about me.

I went to lunch that day and sat by myself as I always did. And I saw that kid walk up with his brown lunch bag.

"Thank you," he said to me and gave me his bag with his lunch in it.

"What is that?" I asked him.

"It is my lunch. You can have it because I would not have it anyway if it was not for you" he said.

I told him I did not want his lunch, but he could sit down and eat it with me if he wanted. He walked around the table and took a seat.

"My name is Malik," he said as he opened his lunch bag. He went on to tell me that kid picked on him every day, so he was glad something happened to him.

"Well, I don't know what happened to him, but I am glad it did since you said he always picks on you," I said to him emphasizing the '*I don't know what happened*' part to make sure he understood that.

My next-door neighbor was my age. Her name was Stephanie, and she was always a quiet person who stayed to herself. We would always speak, but I could not say we were friends or that we talked a lot. After that incident at the bus stop, I was sitting outside on my steps just enjoying the sun and she came over and sat with me.

"I heard about what happened at the bus today," she said to me. I just looked at her and did not respond. She just sat there looking off into space after she said that, not really expecting a response from me.

"Why does God allow bad people to pick on others? Why do people pick on other people that cannot fight back or defend themselves? There are so many kids in this world that feel all alone as if they have nobody to look out for them, nobody to protect them. So, day after day they sit around and take the abuse in silence," she said in this solemn tone.

"What you did today, it was not just a victory for Malik. It was a little piece of joy for every other kid out there just like Malik. They all got a piece of satisfaction, at least this one time, somebody stood up for them. Somebody took on the bully and made them pay," she said as I finally turned to look at her.

I did not speak, I just looked at her as she stared into space while speaking. I was clinging to her words as they sounded as if they were spoken from the heart and past experiences. We just sat there on the steps talking that day until it got dark.

I saw the world differently after that day. I knew the neighborhood I lived in and the things that were happening in the streets. But, before that day I never really watched and saw things that were happening and the vultures and opportunists I lived around.

Stephanie and I were walking home from the bus stop after school, and we saw kids in Old Lady Jones' flowers. Old Lady Jones was an elderly lady who lived alone. She was the one person that planted flowers by their window in the hood.

Kids would call her mean or fear her because she was always sitting in the window looking out over her garden. If a ball or a kid was playing too close to her garden, you would hear her yelling out the window, "Get away from my garden."

This time Old Lady Jones' curtains were closed. This group of kids was pulling her flowers up out of the ground.

We just looked at them. "Why are they doing that?" Stephanie said as I started to cross the street.

She grabbed my arm. "No, leave them alone," she said to me. When I turned back to look at them, they were running away.

I walked across the street and Stephanie followed. I knocked on Old Lady Jones' door and she answered. You could tell she had been crying. "Ms. Jones, some kids were out here in your garden," I told her.

She took a step out of the door and looked over at her garden. "No!" She screamed before she really broke down in tears. "No," she repeated as she looked at me. "Why lord, why?" she said. She then looked at me crying and said, "Thank you," and closed her door.

I walked over to her garden and started trying to pick her flowers. They not only pulled them out of the ground, but they also tore them so there was nothing anybody could do. Stephanie came over to help me.

"My mom told me that Old Lady Jones' daughter died of cancer," she said as we were collecting the flowers.

"She told my mom that when her daughter was dying, she gave her this flower and told her that she would always be with her," Stephanie continued. "Mom said that everybody always thought she was looking out the window at her flowers, but she was really looking out the window talking to her daughter," she said as I paused to listen.

"That was why she was so protective of her garden" I heard Stephanie say as I looked down at these broken pieces of flowers. I could hear her in the house crying but there was nothing more we could do. So we picked up our bags and headed home. Knowing what those flowers meant to her bothered me all night even though I did not know her.

The next day at school, I had a plan. We had a school garden, so I went to the horticulture teacher and told her what happened. And I asked her if I could have one flower to take back to Old Lady Jones and plant in her garden.

The teacher was excited to have me want to do such a thing, so she was eager to give me a flower. She asked me what kind I wanted and made suggestions on which ones I should get and what I needed to do to take care of it. I left there with a beautiful flower for Ms. Jones' garden, hoping this would help remind her of her daughter again.

After school that day, Stephanie and I got off the bus and I had the flower. We were going to plant it in her garden to try and make things right. As we were approaching, we saw police cars and an ambulance near her building. This was the hood, so seeing police cars was nothing unusual.

We realized that they were all around Ms. Jones' place. We rushed over to see what was going on, and just as we got there, we could see them rolling the stretcher out of her house with a white sheet covering it.

"What happened?" I spoke. Her neighbor who was standing next to me told me that Ms. Jones was so depressed about the flowers and losing what she thought was her only connection to her daughter.

"I guess she felt she had nothing else to live for, she died of depression," the neighbor said.

I looked at Stephanie and the flower we brought over. I walked past the caution tape and to her garden. I dug a little hole with my hand and placed that flower in her garden.

"I am sorry, I should have been there. I should have done something," I said as I got off my knees and walked back to my house. Now, I was feeling at least partially responsible for another death.

"I swear, I am never going to stand by and watch things like this again," I said. "I promise," I said as I walked into my house.

CHAPTER 3

BREAKING POINT

Stephanie watched as I left Ms. Jones' house and could see the pain and hurt on my face. She spoke to me, and I kept walking as if she didn't say a word. She didn't try and stop me or run behind me, she just watched. She knew that look and the pain it was hiding.

I went inside the house and straight to my room. Grandmom saw me walk in, she saw the tears and the pain.

"You ok son" she said to me.

"I don't want to talk," I said to her as I kept walking past her and into my room. I shut the door and lay down on my bed crying. How was something like this happening again? Why was God being so cruel to me? Why was God testing me and putting all this death around me? Why was God putting all this guilt on me? Why me?

I sat in the room and my grandmom could hear me crying. She knew that I would need some alone time. She went into the kitchen and started baking as I sat in there contemplating life. I sat up and looked in the mirror crying and thinking.

"Stew baby, I baked some cookies," Grandmom said from the other side of the door. She didn't open the door, she was trying to let me process it the best way I could.

"You want to share some cookies with me," she said.

"No, I just want to be alone" I yelled back.

"OK baby, I am here if you need anything," she said as she took her plate of cookies and walked back to the kitchen. Grandmom sat down in her chair in the kitchen crying. She knew I was in pain and knew there was nothing she could do about it but give me time and space until I was ready to talk.

I saw a razor blade on the dresser as I was sitting there staring at the mirror. That was it, that was put there for a reason. I walked over and grabbed the razor blade off the dresser and went and sat back on the bed.

Here I was looking in the mirror, crying with a razor in my hand. In that mirror, I saw my three-year-old self so innocent and excited walking into the house to share my ice cream with my mom. Ice Cream represents a sense of utopia. Ice cream is happy and joyous. Kids eating ice cream is the epitome of innocence and happiness.

I was walking in with a cone full of innocence, euphoria, and happiness smiling and ready to share this with my mom. I opened the door and there she was lifeless staring at me. I dropped the ice cream in the doorway.

I stood there staring at the ice cream on the floor. It was not a cone full of milk and sugar I just dropped on the floor. I wasn't staring at this wonderful blend of milk, butter, sugar, and eggs that created the most joyous experience for kids all over the world, this joy called ice cream.

I was staring at the innocence and happiness that life had knocked out of the hands of a three-year-old forever. I was looking at the ground at the end of my life as I knew it.

I could see the ice cream in that mirror.

Then I saw a reflection in the mirror of a pair of red and black tennis shoes under my bed. As I looked at those shoes, I saw those boys running away with my dad's bag with our shoes in them.

I looked down and on the back of my hand was blood and a chunk of human flesh. I just looked at this red chunk of matter on my hand. This wasn't dirt, food, or a piece of trash resting on the back of my hand. This was a piece of my dad's brain matter.

I slowly turned to the right to look at my dad laying there. His eyes were wide open looking back at me. He is looking at me as if he was asking for help.

"Help me," I saw in his eyes. "Why didn't you help me" his eyes said to me. There was one stream of blood that captured my attention as if dripping from the bullet hole in his head. I watched as it rolled down his forehead and past his eyes. Past the eyes that were staring at me and were lifeless.

It rolled down the side of his nose. All I could think about was that was the same nose he would take every day as an infant and rub it up against my stomach trying to make me laugh. I would laugh with the innocence of a newborn as he rubbed that nose back and forth across my belly.

Then it rolled past his mouth reminding me of when he had rubbed his nose against my belly enough, he put his mouth on my stomach, took a deep breath, and blew against my stomach. The air rushing from his mouth made the most playful sounds as it vibrated off my belly.

He would raise up, and say, "here I come" and then place his mouth on my belly and blow with all of his force again, making the vibrations even stronger this time, the noise louder and me laughing harder. I would grab his head to push him away as it tickled too much, but only push him far enough away, that he could take a breath and do it again.

I saw the blood roll past his mouth and drip from his chin to the ground. On the ground, I saw a puddle forming. The puddle grew bigger as more and more memories of the times we shared rolled past his eye, followed by his nose, and then his mouth before dumping those memories on the ground; as if they were as worthless as the debris and litter laying in the street.

I looked in the mirror and saw the razor in my hand. I was holding that razor in a hand, a hand still covered in dirt. The same dirt I was digging in planting a flower for Ms. Jones. I could see that flower; it no longer was just her sitting in the window looking at the garden at her daughter.

I was sitting in the window with her. Looking out the window with her. She saw her daughter in those flowers, and I saw my mom and dad. We sat in the chairs and could feel the pain and emptiness that death left behind as we both could only turn to looking at these flowers to try and ease the pain.

I looked at the razor in my hand and turned my other wrist over. The flowers couldn't ease the pain any longer, the pain was too much. My only relief was in the power of this razor.

My grandmom heard a knock on the door. She went to the door, and it was Stephanie.

"Hello Ms. Stewart, I wanted to give him some time alone before I came to check on him," she said to my grandmom.

"Come on in baby, he could probably use you right now," she said as she let her into the house.

"Here are some cookies, you two can share them," giving Stephanie the plate of cookies she tried to give to me earlier.

Stephanie knocked on the door and didn't get an answer. She knocked gently again, and still no response.

"Stew, I am coming in," she said as she began to open the door. She slowly pushed it open and peeked inside first as she came through the door.

She saw me laying on the floor, and I was not moving. She walked in with the plate of cookies and shut the door behind her.

"Stew," she said, still not getting any response.

She walked over to where I was laying, and then she saw the razor in my hand.

"Stew," she said again hoping I would respond.

She started to tear up as she knew the pain I had been experiencing. She walked over to where I was laying and sat down near my head crying. She sat the plate on the ground and gently rubbed my head.

She took the razor out of my hand.

"I can't take it any longer," I finally spoke without moving. She just started rubbing my head. I sat up next to her and looked at the razor she had taken from my hands. Looking at that razor, I broke down and started crying uncontrollably.

She just put her arms around me, pulled me close to her and let me cry on her shoulder. It was tears of all my pain, anger, and feelings soaking her shoulder. That hug, that shoulder, that comfort was everything that I needed at the time. Just her holding me helped me calm down and get it all back together.

"Can you stay?" I asked her.

"Give me a minute," she responded. She got up and grabbed the razor, putting it in her pocket as she walked out of the door.

I am sure my grandmom and her mom would understand the things that were going on and would be ok, I needed them to be ok. I am not sure I would make it through the night without her.

She came back and I was still sitting on the floor in the same spot. She closed the door and sat back down in the same spot.

We both just sat there with our backs against the wall.

"We all have dark secrets, excruciating pain, or other demons inside of us that we have to find somebody to share them with when they become too heavy to bare alone," she said as we sat there.

"You have to promise if it ever becomes too much to carry alone, you will call me and we can work through it together," she said to me.

I just looked at her. She was not judgmental, and I felt like she could relate to the things that I was going through. I felt like she was the only person in the world that truly understood me. The only person that I could open up to emotionally.

"Thank you," I said to her. Just thanking her for understanding. I gave her a blanket and we fell asleep on the floor.

I was partially asleep and could hear grandmom open the door to peek in to check on us. She walked in and just looked at us laying there peacefully. She got emotional knowing all I was going through, but it made her smile to know that I found somebody to be able to share with.

She came over and pulled the covers up over both of us and turned and walked back out of the room. Between Stephanie being there and comforting me, and my grandmom just showing love as only a grandparent could, I fell into a deep sleep.

I was awakened from my sleep as I felt Stephanie jump in her sleep and yell "No." I sat up to see what was going on and she jumped again. "Stop." she said as she was still laying there. I looked at her and realized she was sleeping.

I slid closer to her and put my arms around her to hold her. I could feel her heart racing and her heavy breathing. But, she was still asleep. After I put my arm around her, I could feel her heartbeat slow down. I could feel her breathing become normal again. I guess I was as comforting to her as she was to me.

We woke up the next morning about the same time. We realized we were laying there together, and I was holding her. We both jumped back and looked at each other. "Eww," she said to me.

"Man, you were having a bad dream, so I was just trying to calm you down," I said to her. "Anyway, what were you dreaming about? You sounded scared."

"Nothing, I mean I don't know," she answered as if she was trying to change the subject. It was a Saturday so we could smell grandmom in the kitchen cooking breakfast.

"You hungry," I said as I was getting up to go in the kitchen.

"Sure thing," she said as she got up to follow. The kitchen was filled with the aroma of fresh breakfast and a slight breeze through the house as grandmom had the front door open.

We sat at the table eating and joking, just enjoying breakfast. I saw Stephanie looking out the front door and something caught her attention. Whatever it was wiped the smile off her face. I turned to look out the door to see what had captured her attention. I didn't see anything except a guy getting out of the car.

I looked back at her and saw the laughter and joy was gone.

"What is wrong?" I said as I looked back at the door again to see what it could be.

"Nothing," she said. "It's just my uncle is here. I don't like him," she said as I turned to see him walking up the sidewalk.

"Oh yeah. I see him over there all the time," I said to her as I got a second look at him.

She really must not care for him as he ruined her mood. I wanted to ask her why she didn't like him, but grandmom was there, and I didn't want to have that conversation in front of grandmom.

We enjoyed breakfast and I tried to get the smile back on her face as her uncle disappeared into their next-door apartment. We ate breakfast and went back into my room and started a game of Uno. We played the game and just had fun taking my mind off everything.

We spent most of the morning and early afternoon playing until her mom came knocking on the door. I walked her to the door as her mom was waiting. I saw her looking out the door past her mom.

"Mom, I see Uncle James still here," she said to her mom in a somber tone.

"Yeah, he just taking a nap. He worked over night," her mom told her.

"You about to go somewhere?" she asked her mom. She told her no. She just wanted her to come home to take a bath and change clothes.

"Can I come back afterwards?" she asked.

She showered and was back in an hour. We were sitting in the room and I had to ask her. "Why you don't like your uncle?" I asked her.

"Nothing, I just don't like him. He is not a good person and my mom doesn't see it," she said to me. I didn't press the issue, she answered, and we just moved on. We had a fun evening hanging out, and we convinced my grandmom to let her spend the night again.

We sat up talking all night about anything and everything. I gave her the bed this time and I made myself comfortable on the floor. Grandmom woke me when she came into the room to turn off the tv as we had fallen asleep.

I was falling back to sleep, and it started again. Stephanie started jumping and yelling in her sleep. This time it was much worse than it was the night before. This time I reached up to try and wake her. I startled her, and she jumped up in a panic when I shook her. You could see her sweating this time.

"You had another dream," I said to her explaining why I woke her.

"Oh, I am sorry," she said as she laid back down. "Didn't mean to wake you," she told me.

"No worries," I said as I laid back down to go to sleep.

That weekend took a pretty close relationship we had with one another to a different level. We felt like we could share everything with each other. I felt like she was the friend who could help me control the mental demons I faced.

Stephanie had grown to fill the void in my heart that was left with the death of my mom and dad. I didn't realize how I longed for somebody I knew was going to be there and have my back regardless of the situation. That is how I felt about her, there was this unconditional love that was forming.

We were sitting out on the porch talking and watching cars go by. We were talking about our dreams and the houses we would buy when we were older.

"I'm going to find my husband and we going to get married in this huge church with red and white everywhere," she said to me dreaming of the future.

"You know you not going to be able to get married," I responded to her.

"Every time you meet a guy, I am going to be like that overprotective dad and show up at his house with a gun and put it to his head daring him to mess up," I said laughing.

"That's why I wouldn't even tell you if I met a guy. You would try running them away," she responded to me.

"See that kid. Me and my husband are going to have one just like that. We going to go out and share ice cream together like they are," she said pointing to a man, woman, and a little kid walking down the sidewalk. They looked like the perfect family. Dad, mom, and a little boy walking while eating ice cream.

As we were watching them, the little kid who was about three, tripped and fell dropping his ice cream. The kid got up, looked at his ice cream on the ground, and started crying.

The dad seemed really upset. "what did I tell you about crying?" he yelled at the little kid.

"Don't cry baby," the lady said as she was handing her ice cream to the little kid. You could see the anger on the dad's face. He knocked the ice cream out of the mom's hand.

"Don't give his little crying ass anything," he yelled at her.

Seeing him knock the ice cream from the mom's hand, I stood up. Stephanie grabbed my arm. sit down that is none of our business."

The little boy heard him yell at his mom and started to cry harder.

"I told your ass about crying," the man said to the little kid; hitting the kid across his head with an open hand, knocking the kid down in the street.

"Stop that," the mom said as she reached for the dad's hand.

"Bitch, don't touch me," he said, reaching back to hit the mom with a backhand slap which knocked her to the ground also.

I started having flashbacks. That compartment door in my mind which locked the pain of bullying inside my head had been kicked open by this guy. My blood was beginning to boil and Stephanie could tell it. The thoughts of Mom and Dad were running rampant. The thought of doing nothing like I had done before, and thinking my lack of doing nothing caused Ms. Jones to die was on my mind.

I snatched my arm away from Stephanie.

"No, Stew," Stephanie yelled.

I made a beeline off the porch down the sidewalk. As I was walking toward the street, I picked up a brick lying near the edge of the yard.

"Get y'all asses up," the man was yelling at the mom and kid he had knocked down in the street.

By this time, I had tuned the rest of the world out. It was as if I couldn't hear or see anything except this guy. He was standing there yelling at them with his back to me.

I walked up behind him, took the brick and hit him in the back of his head; knocking him down. He hit the ground and I kicked him.

"Stop hitting on little kids," I said to him, kicking him in his ribs again.

"How does that feel for somebody to hit on you?" I said as I kicked him again, this time in the head. I saw the lady sitting there holding the little boy, not saying anything. She just watched as I kicked him.

I picked up the brick and was walking over to hit him again. Then I felt Stephanie grab me.

"Stop Stew. Stop," she said, holding me. Her grabbing me snapped me out of the rage-filled haze I was in. I looked at Stephanie and then the mom and kid.

"You right," I said to Stephanie. Instead of hitting that man in the head again, I just threw the brick at him; hitting him in the stomach before turning to walk back to my house.

The mom got the little kid to his feet and they walked off together leaving the dad laying in the street, bleeding and battered.

"You know you are going to get in trouble if you keep doing that, no matter how much somebody else is wrong," Stephanie said to me. I knew I couldn't walk around like some street vigilante, but I just lose it sometimes. I feel like I can't control myself or my thoughts when I see certain things.

We saw that man several times after that, but we never saw him again with the lady and kid. Hopefully, that was the day they decided enough was enough, and she left.

All throughout our high school years, Stephanie and I stayed connected at the hip. Nobody saw one without seeing the other. We didn't have many other people we talked to or hung out with except each other.

"You know you ain't ever going to get married," I joked with her as we were walking home.

"I don't want to get married anyway," she said. "I just want to graduate next month and move away from here," she told me.

"You keep saying that. You would leave me? And you always wanted to get married," I said to her.

"I wouldn't leave you, just everybody else. And I don't want to get married. Men are pigs, and I don't ever have to have a man in my life except for a brother like you," she said.

"Ok, you are man-bashing. Time to change the subject," I said in a not-so-joking tone.

We had made it through high school. I had a few incidents in high school where the rage and anger inside revealed itself on a bully or somebody. I actually got suspended from school twice because of it during my high school years.

But, with Stephanie there every step of the way, I was able to steer clear of too many explosions.

After high school Stephanie and I both got hooked up with a job at the post office. We moved in together and it was great. She was the sibling I never had and my best friend. I could still hear her screams at night sometimes. I told her she needed to go to a sleep doctor to stop those dreams.

We had been out of school about four years and doing ok for ourselves. It was the 4th of July weekend and

Stephanie's family was having a cookout at her cousin's house. It was the typical holiday cookout and we were having a great time.

"Where is the bathroom, Steph?" I said to her as I had too much to drink and needed to go bad.

"I'll show you. I need to go also," she said as she got up. We went to the bathroom and tried to open the door; however, it was locked.

"Occupied," we heard somebody say as we smelled what was coming out of the bathroom.

"Oh no. I've got to go real bad and he is going to be in there a minute," I said to Stephanie.

"There's another one upstairs in my Aunt's room. Let's go," she said, heading up the stairs.

We rushed up the stairs with Stephanie leading me into the bedroom. When we walked into the room, she saw her little niece on the bed crying. We both stopped at the door as she was crying.

"What is wrong Kenya?" Stephanie said to her. Before she could answer, her uncle walked out of the bathroom.

"Nothing is wrong with her. She just has an upset stomach. Right?" he said, trying to get the little girl to confirm.

I saw the look on Stephanie's face when he walked out of the bathroom. It was the same uncle and the same look she had every time she saw him.

"Are you OK?" she asked her niece again.

"I told you she was fine," her uncle said. "Now let's go," he said to the niece who was still crying.

"She is not going anywhere with your sick ass," Stephanie said to him, angrier than I have ever heard her speak.

"Fine, stay y'all asses here," he said while walking out of the bedroom before heading down the stairs.

Stephanie rushed over and grabbed her. She got her up and held her. "Did he touch you?" Stephanie said to her. That caught me off guard. I was not expecting her to say that.

The little girl didn't say anything, she just kept crying. Stephanie told her she didn't have to be afraid to feel safe. She could tell her. I was listening to this not knowing what to make of it.

"You have to speak up and let me know if he touched you," she said to her. "Listen, I was young like you when he first touched me. He never stopped. I never had anybody to turn to. So you can tell me." she said to the girl. That statement froze me in my tracks.

"You said what?" I asked Stephanie.

"Yes, he used to molest me as a kid. I am not going to sit and let him do it to somebody else," she said. The little girl broke down crying harder after Stephanie said that.

Hearing that took me to a mental place I had never been. I saw my mom's dead body hanging. I saw a kid shoot my dad. But this was a completely different level of anger and hatred. Then I started thinking of the day at breakfast when she saw him outside the door and her entire mood changed.

I started thinking about all of the nights, I heard her scream or jump and thought it was a bad dream. I started thinking about the one person who means more to me than anybody on earth. Stephanie had been sexually abused, carried the pain for years, and I did nothing about it.

Stephanie looked up and saw the look in my eyes. The look of death. The look which was void of humanity. She had seen the look before several times. When she saw that particular look, she always grabbed me to calm me, but it never worked.

I turned to walk back down the stairs. This time, she didn't grab me. She didn't try to stop me as I headed down the stairs with a level of rage I had never experienced before. I had reached the state again where I tuned out the entire world. I couldn't see or hear anything but visions of my mom and dad. This time I had visions of this guy touching Stephanie. A tear formed in my eye.

I grabbed a baseball bat sitting by the door. He was seated outside at the table as if nothing had happened. I walked toward him gripping the bat. I was holding the bat so tight, I could feel the blood being squeezed out of my fingers and them turning colors.

Stephanie ran out the door behind me. Once at the table, I took a swing with the bat, hit him on his side, and knocked him out of the chair to the ground. As he fell, his feet knocked the card table over, and others at the table scrambled to get clear.

I held the bat over my head and swung down as hard as I could, hitting him in the stomach. I could hear voices and noise but I couldn't make out anybody's voice or what they were saying, except for Stephanie.

I heard her say "No Ma. He's been molesting me for years and now he touched Kenya." I threw the bat down and began punching him as he lay on the ground. Some family members ran over to break it up, and Stephanie picked up the bat.

She turned to them. "Nobody is about to stop him. Nobody is about to help him," she said as everybody paused while she raised the bat towards them. Nobody was really in a rush to save him. Nobody was really interested in stopping me from beating him.

I heard Stephanie's voice echo in my head "he been molesting me." Her words fueled my rage to continue punching. I got off him and went over to the barbeque grill to grabbed a knife off the grill. I walked back over and kicked him. "Don't you ever touch an innocent little girl again," I stated, kicking him in the face.

I took the knife and stabbed him right in his groin. "You won't ever use this to hurt another little girl," I screamed at him. Getting up, I kicked him in the face again, and saw his tooth and a mouth full of blood fly across the yard.

Then I heard the only voice that was audible to me.

"OK, Stew. Let's go," I could hear Stephanie say. I dropped the knife; she grabbed my arm and pulled me back. I had gone to a place where I had never been before. Thinking about him molesting Stephanie became my breaking point.

CHAPTER 4

INDECENT PROPOSAL

All actions have consequences. Being unable to control my emotions this time could cost me dearly. The ambulance arrived at the house along with the police, as they were responding to a report of a man being stabbed. Right after the incident, Stephanie and I left.

"Stew, I think you went too far this time," she said to me as I was driving. "I just thought you would beat him up or something, I did not think you would stab him. What if he dies?"

I did not say a word as I was driving, and she went on continuing to express her concern about the things that transpired. As she was talking, her phone rang. It was her mother.

"Steph, the police want you and Stew to come back to the house," I could hear her say through the phone. Stephanie just looked at me. "Mom, I will call you back," she said to her mom and hung up.

"So, what are you going to do," she said to me. "You know if you go back, they probably are going to arrest you for assault. You do not have to go back; you can let some time pass until I can talk to my uncle to make sure he does not press charges."

"I am going back," I said to her as I hit a U-turn in the street. I was innocent, at least I felt as if what I did was understandable. Plus, he would never press charges, because that would mean his dirt would have to come out also.

We turned the corner to the house and see three police cars there but no ambulance. We park and walk up the sidewalk to the house. We approach the front door as the police officers are walking out.

"Hello, are you Derek Stewart," the police officer said to me.

"Yes, I am sir," I responded.

He grabbed my arm, "Derek Stewart, you are under arrest for the murder of James Jenkins," I heard him say and it seemed like the entire world stopped spinning at that moment.

"Murder?" Stephanie said in total shock.

"Yes, Mr. Jenkins died on the way to the hospital," the police officer responded.

Hearing that he died on the way to the hospital I was in shock. I was standing there in handcuffs about to be taken to jail. But I was conflicted. I was truly upset that I was about to go to jail tonight and not home. On the other hand, I had little or no remorse for his fate. I was thinking anybody that would do that to kids, they deserve whatever happens to them.

I know, killing another person is not right, not justified. But seeing the things I saw with death as a kid, some people simply deserve to experience severe pain in their lives, and if they happen to die, they should have thought about that when they did unthinkable things to innocent people that couldn't protect themselves.

I did not say another word on the way to the precinct. They booked me in and threw me in a holding cell. I looked around this crowded cell full of Black men of all ages as I found a place on the bench to sit down.

"Welcome to the Dekalb County Hotel," some guy said to me joking. I just looked at him. It was quite the mixture of men to be in one room together. Jail is the one place that humbled everybody. As I looked around the room, I saw a well-dressed, well-groomed black man in what looked like a custom suit, sitting on the same bench a few feet from an older guy that looked like he was homeless.

There was a guy in there with a tank top on the ground doing push-ups, showing off his bulging arms, just a few feet away from another that was obviously gay. This was a true melting pot, in this room, everybody was an equal no matter how much money you had or did not have. How educated you were or not.

You could see some in here that looked as if it were no big deal and some that looked as if they were a nervous wreck. I just sat there and watched.

"Hey, guard come over here and let me out dammit. I know you hear me. When I get out, I am going to fuck your momma," this guy said as he stood by the door beating on the steal door. Everybody was ignoring him.

"He has been like this all night; they need to take him to the psych ward," the guy sitting next to me said.

"Stewart, somebody here to see you," I heard the guard say. He handcuffed me and took me into a room where I was met by my attorney. I told Stephanie to find me a good attorney.

We sat down and he explained everything to me. He told me that I was not going to be granted bond right now and I would have to stay here until a pre-trial. The magnitude of everything was starting to hit me and the possibility that I could be going to jail for a long time.

I had time to sit and think about things leading up to my arraignment hearing. Lots of things were going through my mind, including the nightmares that this guy caused Stephanie to have. I was set to meet with my attorney to discuss his plan and arraignment.

He explained that it was going to be an uphill battle for me in court, but we had a chance if we got in front of a sympathetic jury and laid out all the details that led up to it. He told me about what would happen at the arraignment and what his plan would be.

I stopped him. "I want to plead no contest."

"Why, you have a real chance to beat this case or at least get lesser charges," he said. I put my elbow on the table, slid my chair up close to the table, and told him to listen carefully.

"We will not go to trial. I will not have Stephanie re-live the things that monster did to her in public for everybody to hear. I will not do that to her and that is the end of the discussion."

He paused for a minute. He sat back and crossed his arms.

"I totally understand but listen to me. I promise you that we will not go to court, and she will never have to testify, but a no-contest today is not the way," he explained. He went on to tell me that we could just plead not guilty today, and he would collaborate with the prosecutor to get a plea deal and a reduced charge before the court so Stephanie would not have to testify.

I agreed to that, and we called for the guards to get me. As I was walking out, I paused and said to him, "Stephanie does not need to know anything about this." I did not want to put her in the position of thinking she had to testify to help me.

And that day I accepted my fate. The attorney got the prosecutor to agree to manslaughter and the judge sentenced me to twelve years. That was worth it to not make Stephanie re-live those terrible things out in public for the world to hear.

With that, I was sent off to spend the next twelve years of my life in prison.

Being in a cell with Mark was the best thing that could have happened in prison. Like my friendship that developed with Stephanie, I developed a similar type of bond with Mark. I felt like he was a person I trusted and that understood me.

We both were good people that accepted our fate and responsibility for the things we did that landed us in jail. We both knew better and knew there were demons we must face head-on to do better in life. I respected Mark because he had faced those drug demons and beat them.

I was walking out of the prison shower when I heard some commotion in the stall area. In prison, you learn to keep to yourself and mind your business. So, I was going to mind my business and walk out of there. As I walked by the stall, I noticed two guys and what looked like they were attempting to rape this small young kid.

But this was not any of my business, so I kept walking. As I got to the door, I heard the kid say "Stop, somebody please help me." Those words stopped me in my tracks. "Help me." That phase haunts me as I sat idly and did not help my mom, my dad, or Ms. Jones.

I stood in the doorway thinking to myself that this was prison, and this was none of my business. Keep walking out of this door, do not look back. Though my mind was telling me to keep walking, my consciousness would not let me move.

I turned around and walked back to the stall.

"Leave him alone," I said, catching the two guys off guard.

"Get your ass out of here and mind your business," one of the guys said to me.

"I said, leave him alone," I repeated firmly.

I then had both of their attention as they let the kid go and turned to face me. When they let him go, he scrambled to rush out of the stall and out of the bathroom.

"What, are you some type of Captain Save-A-Hoe or something. Your little hoe done left you all alone," the other guy said as he walked up to me.

I felt that rage building inside thinking of the uncle molesting Stephanie. No innocent person should experience the pain of sexual abuse, not even a prisoner.

I did not flinch as I found myself standing face to face with these two men, all alone in the bathroom. We were nose to nose, and you could feel the tension and the potential for violence in the air. Once again, my conscious was about to put me in a bad position.

It was two of them, so I figured I better strike first because this was prison and there was no backing down from this standoff. It was going to be handled right now, or they would come back and catch me off-guard. Either way, this was going to result in a violent encounter.

Almost like a reflex, I grabbed this guy by the back of his head and head-butted him in the face knocking him to the ground. The other guy punched me knocking me backwards. I regrouped and charged him tackling him as the back of his head hit a toilet. I delivered three punches to his face before I realized that he was knocked out.

I got up and turned my attention to the other guy who had gotten up and was standing there holding his nose as it was bleeding profusely.

About that time, Mark walked in. After looking at the scene "Stew, what the hell have you done" he said to me. Hearing his voice snapped me out of the rage-filled trance. I turned and looked at him.

"Nothing, they slipped in the shower," I said to him as I walked out of the door. Mark turned and looked at the two of them, shook his head, and followed me out of the door.

When I walked back into my cell, Mark was doing his usual thing, laying down, reading a book. He put his book down and sat up on his bed.

"Stew, I am going to talk to Dr. Owens. You need to see her more than once a week for a private session, he stated. "You are a good dude with a good heart, but you are not coping well with some things in your past, I want to be there to help you get past that."

I looked at him and thought about it. Though I know these are rage-filled moments in my life, at no point do I feel like I ever regret it afterwards. I never feel like I have done anything to anybody that did not deserve it.

"Mark, can I say something, and you not judge me," I said to him as I was thinking about sharing my thoughts. He nodded as if he was waiting for me to speak.

"What if I do not want to forget the pain? What if I do not want to ever forget those things? What if I do not regret anything I have done, in fact, I may even feel good about the things I have done because all of those people deserved it," I said to him waiting for him to tell me how crazy I was.

Mark laid back down on the bed and crossed his legs as I waited for him to respond.

"Stew, I cannot tell you what in life your mission is and what is going to make you happy. And if going through life as some vigilante on a mission makes you happy, just be prepared for the consequences that come with it, knowing it will not end with a family living behind a white picket fence," he stated as he picked his book back up.

I had never looked at it like that. Never looked at it as being a vigilante out here saving the weak and vulnerable. But I think I can accept that.

Word got out around the prison that if you were bullying or picking on a weaker person, do not do it around me. I had garnered the respect and the healthy fear of everybody in prison.

That is why everybody was curious about what would happen with the new prisoner coming in. I stayed away from TV and the news, but everybody was aware of the politician recently convicted. He was an elected official in a small city. This sick person built a torture chamber in his basement, where he would kidnap, sexually assault, and kill young boys and girls.

A sexual predator does not last well in prison and is placed in protective custody for their own safety. I just knew that I needed to stay away from him, I was not sure how I would react if I saw him in person and looked him in the eyes.

Unfortunately for this guy, one of his victims was the niece of one of the guards. This guy could not have any worse luck than that. I was in the bathroom shaving and everything seemed a little too peaceful for jail.

A guard walked in with a prisoner and stood behind me.

"Stew, this guy raped and killed my seven-year-old niece," the guard said. I just looked at my reflection in the mirror. This time I saw it. I saw my eyes become glassy and red. I saw the rage coming over me. I saw this guy's reflection in the mirror and all I could think about was a sweet little seven-year-old crying out and begging for somebody to help her.

The guard turned and walked away. I heard the guy say "What are you doing," toward the guard. Prison has its own way of administering justice and fate had it that this guy would be put in this situation with me, to be forced to understand the ramifications of his actions.

I turned punching this guy in the face, knocking him back against the wall.

"Little kids," I said to him as I punched him again. I had completely lost control of any rational thoughts. I beat him unconscious. I grabbed him by the arm and began to drag him out of the bathroom. At this point, I had no rational thoughts.

I dragged his lifeless body out of the bathroom and down the hall. All the prisoners could see this, and they all began to yell, almost cheering and encouraging brutality. I dragged him to my cell where Mark was in there lying on his bed reading.

"I told you not to bring any trouble to this cell he said," as he briefly looked away from his book long enough to say that. I pulled this guy into the cell and shut the door locking it. I grabbed some bed sheets and tore them into strips. I used those strips to tie this guy up to the toilet seat.

I could feel the rage inside of me growing thinking about all the innocent little kids whose lives this guy took. I could picture their faces running through my mind, one after another. I punched him and could hear the bones in his jaw break and his scream.

People were rushing to my cell to see. The guards, the prisoners, they knew what they had done. They knew what the result would be.

Mark laid there unphased by it all, and never put his book down.

"Stew, have you thought about what you are doing and the consequences for it," he said to me, still holding his book.

"He deserves whatever happens for raping and killing little innocent kids," as I punched him again.

"OK," Mark said as he put his nose back in his book as if I was not beating a guy to death two feet away from him. You could hear the alarms go off as guards were rushing up to the cell. They were pushing their way through prisoners to get to my cell door.

"Everybody get back," one guard said. "Back to your cells."

I could hear the guards calling my name. I could hear them telling me to stop. But they were in no rush to open the cell, they were complicit and let me administer prison justice to this piece of human trash.

I punched him repeatedly. Each time the back of his head bounced off the steel toilet. The rage just kept building and I just kept punching. The guards finally opened the door and rushed in. As I heard the door open, I just laid on the cell floor with my arms spread apart.

I was laying there facing this bleeding and lifeless body as I was staring into his face. As the guard was handcuffing me, the other rushed over to him.

"I think he is dead," I heard him say. My first thought was not that I killed a man. My first thought was that he got off easy. He should not be able to die. He should be tortured and punished day after day for the things he did to those kids. A quick death was not justice, it was sparing him of the agony and pain he deserved.

At the point that the guards were leading me out of my cell, Mark's words to me about suffering the consequences and how this was going to end, they started to hit home. I realized I had just killed a man out in the open in jail. I was about to spend the rest of my life in jail.

I was banished to solitary confinement. I was to sit in this individual cell for 23 hours a day for the next two years. Spending time in isolation with no real interaction with others makes you reflect upon life and your decisions. I realized that I wanted to punish predators and bullies, but there was no end game. I was going to end up like I am now, in jail for life.

I spent the next few months working out in my cell ten hours a day. I had nothing else to do, so I focused on my body and physical condition. The days started running together and before I realized it, I had been in solitary confinement for 10 months. I had not seen Mark, had not talked to Stephanie, and did not get a chance to attend sessions with Dr. Owens.

I could see my body changing. I would guess I have put on about twenty pounds of muscle since I'd been in solitary. Jail is meant to reform people, but all they have done now is created a bigger, stronger version of me.

I heard the guard at my cell. This was strange because nobody ever comes by here for anything except mealtimes.

"Today is your lucky day, somebody is here to see you," he said. That confused me, I was in solitary confinement, and I was not allowed any guests or visitors. Who would have the ability to get me out of the cell to see them?

I walked into the room and was shocked at what I saw. It was Dr. Owens sitting in the room. I just looked at her as I walked in and took a seat.

"What power you got that you were able to get me out of there to come and have a session with you," I asked her.

"Well, I am not here for a therapy session. I am here to do an evaluation and talk to you," she said to me.

"Evaluation for what," I said to her.

"Based on our conversation and my evaluation, you may be able to get released back into gen pop and out of confinement," she explained to me.

That sounded like music to my ears. I had my share of solitary for now and need to get out of there. I am curious as to why this is happening, but I am not going to look a gift horse in the mouth.

I spent about an hour in there with Dr. Owens. She asked me some strange questions, and even though I was trying to get out, I tried to be honest about my thoughts and answered her questions truthfully. After the meeting, the guards came back and led me to my cell.

A few days later, the guards came with the news I was hoping to hear. They got me and led me back to the general population and my old cell.

"I see nothing has changed since I been gone," I said to Mark as he was laying down reading as they let me in the cell.

Mark looked at me "Welcome back, and I see you been spending your time bulking up, you put on some weight bro," he said commenting on my new physique.

"Man, I am going to say this again, not like you listened the first time. But do not bring any trouble to this cell. I am only a few weeks away from getting an early release," he said to me.

I was excited to hear that his visit before the parole board went well and he was about to get an early release. He was a good guy that made a mistake at a different time in his life and deserved a second chance that he earned.

It was great to spend the night up and just talking to another person. You never knew how much you appreciate the presence of another human being until you cannot have human interaction anymore. Mark put the books down and indulged me with conversation all night, he knew how much it meant to be back and able to talk to somebody.

I promised him, I was going to try and spend more time in my cell until his release. If I stayed away from too many people, I would be able to avoid any triggering events that send me into a violent rage. And did not want to jeopardize his release date, because I lost my cool on somebody.

And then it happened, Mark got the word that he was being released. It was a bittersweet moment for me because he was the only person other than Stephanie that I ever bonded with. But I want him to go about his life and be a happy productive citizen.

A few weeks had passed since Mark was released. He had been back up to visit me a couple times since then and brought a book for me to read each time. My visitors were pretty routine. Stephanie would visit me on Saturday mornings and Mark would come on Sundays.

"Stewart, you got a visitor," the guard came to my cell and told me. I stopped reading the book that Mark had given me and stood up. I was curious as to who was coming to visit me. Nobody had ever visited me, but Stephanie, and Mark and they come on weekends, but this was Wednesday.

I walked into the room and saw a Black man dressed in a suit and I had never seen this man in my life. What on earth did this stranger want from me and how did he get on my visitors' list to see me.

"Do you know who I am," the man said to me after I sat down.

"No, I cannot say I do."

"I am sure you have a lot of questions, but after we talk, you will have a better understanding."

I was listening carefully to hear what it was this strange man had to say.

"First thing is, I was never here. There will not be a record of me being here and once I am gone, the things I am about to offer you are gone forever, as you will not be able to find me ever again."

What was this man here to offer me? My curiosity had peaked about this mystery man. He was powerful enough to get into prison to see me, and by his words, he will disappear into thin air when he leaves.

"I am listening," I said to him.

"Second thing, regardless of what you decide today, nothing we discuss here today will ever leave this room. Even if you decide you do not want to accept my offer, sharing anything said in this room with anybody could be fatal to you and the people you love."

He went on to tell me they had reviewed my entire record, down to my suspensions from school.

"I am here because based on your history, you are an ideal candidate for a program that I am leading," he said to me. My interest was piqued now as to why I was a candidate for his program and what program in prison would be interested in me.

"You seem to have spent most of your life exacting revenge on bad people, people that needed bad things to happen to them," he started. "But you were doing those things as a criminal committing crimes against others."

"I lead a covert squad that could use your skill, desire, and ability to serve justice on individuals or groups that the hands of justice are having trouble dealing with." Now he had gotten my attention. "You can walk out of here today a free man, but you belong to me if you accept this offer. You do what I say, when I say, and how I say it. Nobody ever says a word about what you do and why. You will be justly compensated for your work but being released from prison early is a benefit of the job that you can't put a price tag on."

"What exactly is it that you want me to do," I said to him.

He opened a folder he had on the desk.

"Same thing you did to city councilman Larry Craig," as he dropped a picture of the dead body of the guy I killed in prison.

"Same thing you did to Jimmy Lewis and Ronald Parker," as he dropped a picture of the beaten and bloodied two guys, I beat for trying to rape that young kid in prison.

"Same thing you did to James Jenkins," as he dropped a picture of Stephanie's uncle's dead body.

"Do I need to continue," he said to me looking down at his folder which looked like it had lots of other papers in it.

"So are you saying you want to hire me to kill people," I said to him.

"Not at all, we want to use you to help the wheels of justice turn," he said to me.

"Let me make sure I understand. You are going to get me out of jail today and all I must do in return; is the same things that got me here and I can do it with no consequences," I asked.

"Let me make something perfectly clear. I do not exist. You do not exist. This team does not exist. If you get caught, you will end up back here because this team and this conversation never happened," he emphasized.

I took in everything he said to me. It sounded too good to be true, but the thought of being released from prison was all that was on my mind.

"How long do I have to think about it," I asked him.

He picked up the pictures that were on the table and grabbed his folder.

"Right now, you have about another 30 seconds. Once I walk out the door, so does your freedom forever," he said to me.

He gathered his things, stood up, and walked toward the door.

"Guard," he said calling for the guard to come and let him out.

The guard opened the door, and he walked out without saying a word. My mind was racing with thoughts of everything he said. Thoughts of the things I have done in my past and the things he said he wanted me to do.

Just as the door was about to close, "I will do it. Count me in," I said.

CHAPTER 5

GHOST SQUAD

As he walked out the door, I asked myself *'what the hell have I gotten myself into.'* I have been offered a 'get out of jail free' card and not given any time to ask questions or understand what was involved. But why would I care? *Nothing they are offering could be worse than sitting in a jail cell for the rest of my life*, I thought.

The guard walked in to escort me back to my cell. As I walked, I observed the bars, the stench of jail, the depressing view of men standing there behind those gray steel bars. Past the cafeteria area, seeing the food most would consider inhumane. Past the community showers which were a reminder of how I had not experienced a second of privacy since first walking through these doors.

A smile came across my face, I got an opportunity to leave all of this behind. An opportunity to just start over again on the outside. I cannot wait to call Stephanie to tell her I am coming home. I also needed to call my guy Mark, to let him know I am coming home. But I remembered he told me that none of this happened, so I could not tell anybody. If I got out early, what would I tell them?

I got back to my cell and just laid down. I lay there looking at the concrete ceiling. Looking at these concrete walls and those steel gray bars they call a door. How these bars have taken so much from me, not just in terms of years, but in the sense of humanity.

I could not sleep that night thinking about that conversation and if any of it was real. Who could I talk to? What would I tell them? I could not make sense of any of it, but the thought of freedom was exhilarating.

As I was lying in bed, a guard came by and slid a note into the cell. I looked at the envelope lying on the floor. I walked over and picked it up off the cell floor and opened it. There was a piece of paper inside the envelope, the only thing written on it was "Be ready at 8 am."

That seemed very cryptic. There was a real level of mystery with everything that was going on. I had to admit though, the mystique around it all was thrilling. I spent the rest of the night lying there counting down the hours until 8 am.

I could not sleep at all that night anticipating the next morning. It had to be about 5 or 6 in the morning when I finally fell asleep. I was awakened by a commotion in the jail.

I sat up as it sounded like a riot was going on outside. I walked to my door to look outside to see what all the commotion was.

It seemed like they were outside my cell rioting. My first thought was that I was leaving here in minutes, and now this is happening. I was not leaving my cell and jeopardizing my release.

As I was standing there, a guy came to my cell door.

"Let's go," he said. I looked at him dressed in inmate clothing. I had no idea who he was and where he wanted me to go, but I was not leaving my cell. I was waiting for them to come and get me so I could walk out of this place.

"No man, I am good. I am not leaving this cell," I said to this guy.

He looked at me. "It is 8 am. Let's go," he said.

That confused me. Was this a coincidence that he mentioned 8 am? I am sure they did not send another prisoner to get me. I was not leaving this cell. I just stood there looking at him.

"The note said to be ready at 8 am, right," he said, looking around, encouraging me to hurry up. Handing me a gray hoodie, he said, "Put this on."

That was confirmation he knew about the note. He knew they were coming to get me at 8 am. "Oh damn! Guess

I should be following him," I thought as I threw on the hoodie and walked out the cell.

"Follow me, do exactly as I say, and keep up," the guy said to me.

He took off running down the hall. I paused before thinking, *"he said to keep up."* Then I started running behind him to catch up. He stopped at the end of the hall and peeked around the corner. There was commotion all over the cell as inmates were fighting and burning things.

This did not look like I was walking out of jail. this started to look like I was breaking out. I was expecting a guard to get and walk me out the front door.

"what is going on?" I asked as he peeked around the corner.

"Don't ask questions, just do as I tell you," he said. "Let's go," he said as he took off running down the hall again. I stayed close to him as we approached the guard station and he stopped again. Peeking inside the guard station, we stood off to the side of the door.

The guard walked out the door and he hit him on the back of the head; knocking him unconscious. He grabbed the keys from the guard's hip.

"Let's go," he said, running into the guard station door. I looked back at the commotion in the jail before running behind him. He buzzed the door to let us out on the other side of the guard station. As that door opened, he peeked around the corner to see if there was anybody in the hall.

The hall was clear, prompting him to take off running again. This time I did not hesitate. I ran with him, stayin close behind. There was only one additional security door separating the jail from the outside. We got to the door, and he searched for the key.

After finding the correct key, he opened the door; thereafter, we ran out the door through the lobby. Exiting the lobby doors, we continued to run into the parking lot. A A red Honda Accord was idly running in the parking lot while a man sat inside.

"Get in the front," he said to me. My heart raced s I came to realize we were breaking out of prison. I got in the car and shut the door. To my surprise, the driver was the same guy who came to the prison to meet with me.

The other guy jumped in the back seat. He hit the gas and the car sped out of the parking lot. I turned to look back and saw the prison behind me. Neither guy said anything, and I did not know what to say so we drove in silence.

We left the prison and drove to Decatur without stopping. We got off at the Memorial Drive exit before they pulled into an old, abandoned shopping center. They pulled around the back of the building. There was nothing back there. I was concerned as to why we were pulling up behind an abandoned shopping center. I wanted to ask why we broke out of prison. I thought they were getting me out legally.

"Why are we here?" I said to them.

A rope came over my head and around my neck As Iasked the question. He pulled the rope tighter, choking me. I tried to grab the rope to loosen its grip around my neck. That did not work as the guy was pulling it too tightly.

This was all a set-up. Somebody did all this, just to get payback for something I had done to somebody. Maybe it was the guy in jail. Maybe it was Stephanie's cousin. How was I so foolish to fall for it? Now I am about to pay for it with my life.

I reached for the other guy in the driver's seat. Tried to grab him, but he knocked my hands down. I had to get this rope from around my neck. So, I again tried to pull the rope free in order to breathe a little. That was not working either.

I tried to reach over the seat to grab the guy. I could feel him just outside of my reach as he pulled harder and harder on the rope around my neck. I kicked the dashboard as I was trying to get enough leverage to free myself from this rope.

I could feel myself gagging and losing consciousness. I could not grab him, and I could not loosen the grips of the rope around my neck. I was struggling, trying to free myself to no avail. It was not working, and I was slowly fading. Everything was getting darker.

I could feel myself losing the strength to fight him off. My arms fell. I was done fighting. Everything went black.

The next thing I recall, I was sitting in a chair as they threw a bucket of water in my face. I woke up to see these same two guys standing in front of me. I tried to jump up and attack them, only to realize I was tied to a chair.

"What the hell! Let me loose," I yelled as I struggled to free my arms and legs from the constraints. My mind was racing, trying to figure out how I could escape. Trying to figure out how I could make it out of here alive. These guys are obviously trying to torture and kill me.

"Who sent you?" I said, receiving no response.

"The first lesson you need to learn is : Never let your guard down. You could be dead now," he said to me.

"Nobody sent us. You agreed to join us. But, I am not sure you are ready or aware of what we are asking of you," he stated.

"Technically, you are a fugitive. You've just escaped from prison," the other guy stated.

"We will train you, teach you how to survive, and live off the grid."

"You will do what we say, when we say, and ask no questions. Your old life, friends, and family no longer exist. They are liabilities to you at this point," the guy stated.

"This is not what I was expecting," I said to him.

"This is very simple. You do what we say, or we walk out of here and call the police to advise them of where they can find an escaped prisoner," he said rather nonchalantly. "The decision is yours."

"How does this work?" I said to them.

"You do what we say. We will tell you what you need to know when you need to know it. If you do not complete your mission, try to run, or let us down in any way, you will be returned to jail to spend the rest of your life, including the additional escape charge that will be added," he explained.

"And understand, if you tell anybody about what we are doing here, you will wish you were going back to jail, because we will hunt you down and kill you," he said as he looked me in my face.

I realized there was no turning back at this point. I complied with them. My only thoughts were of my desire to reach out to Stephanie. She would be worried to death over my escape from prison.

They pulled out a fully automatic machine gun and set it up on a stand ten feet directly in front of me.

"Can you point that somewhere else?" I stated as he was setting it up.

"Your second lesson: Never panic regardless of the situation," he said as he finished setting up the gun.

"When I pull this lever, the floor between you and that door will drop. There will be a six-foot gap between you and this side of the room. You will have thirty seconds to get from there to here because in thirty seconds, this machine gun will go off, killing everything on that side of the room," he explained to me.

"By the way, we are 15 floors up. It is over one hundred and thirty feet down if you fall. All you have to do is escape from that chair, and pull this lever to simply walk back across this room out of the line of fire. Time is starting now," he said as the other guy sprayed a full can of mace on my face.

"Thirty seconds," I heard him say.

I was choking and could not breathe. I was trying to catch my breath from the mace, and I could not see. My vision was blurred as he sprayed the mace directly into my eyes. I was in full panic mode.

I was tied to this wooden chair, having trouble breathing, and could not see. I was fifteen floors up with a machine gun about to start shooting at me any moment.

I kept kicking and pulling my arm, but they were not being freed from the chair. I realized time was ticking. I could sit there panicking and get blasted in a few seconds or figure a way out of here. I jerked at the arms of the chair again and there was no movement.

I then thought to myself, this is a wooden chair. I saw the clock in front of me hit twenty seconds. I jerked again at the arm of the chair to no avail. Eighteen seconds remaining. Then I thought, *'wooden chair'*. Standing up, I slammed the chair back down as hard as I could. I could hear it crack. But my arms and legs were still securely tied to the chair.

Fourteen seconds remaining. I stood up and slammed it down again. Again, I heard the chair crack, but not enough because I was still tied up. Ten seconds remained. I needed to do it again, harder.

One more time, up and down hard. The chair crumbled, breaking into pieces. One arm of the chair fell off and a leg broke. I reached over in an attempt to untie my other arm. Six seconds.

Loosening that arm, I reached down to untie my leg. Five seconds left.

Now I just need to pull this lever. I got to the lever with three seconds to spare.

I pulled. Nothing happened. Two seconds. I pulled it again. Nothing happened. One second. The lever was not working. I did not have enough room to run, let alone jump across a six-foot gap.

Wait, a six-foot gap. I looked down and all I saw was concrete walls over a hundred feet straight down. The clock hit zero and I jumped off the floor, fifteen floors up. I heard the gun going off as bullets were flying mere inches from my head.

I would fall to my death if this did not work. My hands touched one side of the wall. I pressed my feet against the other side of the wall. I was now a human wedge, nothing but two hands on one wall and two feet on another keeping me from falling to a sure death.

I could feel my hands sweating and felt as if I was losing grip. I could not lose grip. There is only one magazine in the machine gun. I just needed to hold on for about twenty seconds longer before the clip was empty.

I could hear the bullets glancing off the walls above me. Looking below I saw nothing but concrete and death. I had to hold on. It was indeed a matter of life or death. And then I heard a click. That was it, the clip was empty.

Now, I needed to scale this wall up to get out of here. One foot at a time. One hand at a time. I scaled up the wall to the top. I reached the top, and slowly, methodically climbed out of there onto the floor. I walked out of the door to see the guys sitting in chairs.

"Looks like you made it," one of them said to me.

"So, if I would have died, you would have just sat in here watching TV as I was dying in the room next door?" I asked them as my eyes still burn from the mace.

"If you couldn't make it out of there, you would be of no use to us; therefore, we would have had to kill you anyway," the guy in the red hoodie said.

"I am going through all of this, and I do not even know your names," I frustratedly said to them.

"I am Red," said the guy in the red hoodie.

"I am Command," said the other guy. "You do what I say, when I say. Red is my second in charge," he continued.

Looking down at my hoodie, I jokingly remarked, "So I guess I am Gray." Using my shirt sleeve, I wipe my eyes again. They just looked at me. "wait, I am Gray for real?"

"Enough of that. You have a lot of training to do. Go wash your face so we can go."

I spent the next two weeks in some of the most intense covert operations training, which was a cross between an army special force training and street fighting. I was bloodied; almost quitting several times. They constantly stressed the mission, each day and during each training exercise. They bombarded me with images of molested kids, abused women, and beaten elders. The anger I felt motivated me to keep going.

But the one thing I missed was Stephanie. I wanted to reach out to her. I am sure she is hurt, thinking I escaped, and had not reached out. I had spent every day in training exercises with no time to reach out to her if I could.

I had free time, so I decided to go by Stephanie's place just to see if things were ok with her. I knew I was not supposed to communicate with her, but I wanted to somehow let her know that I was ok. I wanted to let her know I did not escape from prison. But how could I let her know any of this? I was told I could not reach out to any people from my past.

I drove to her neighborhood and parked down the street. I turned the car off and watched her as she sat on the porch talking to somebody. I could not reach out to her, but it was good just to see her face and know she was doing ok. I sat there thinking about all the things we went through together as kids, the fun times we had. I could only imagine what she thought about me right now.

I started the car and pulled off down the street. Stephanie saw the car passing by. I pulled my hat down on my head in an attempt to hide my face. I could see her looking at the car.

I was not sure if she were able to recognize me, but I could see her watching the car intently as I drove past.

Stephanie stood up and watched the car drive away. Looking in the rearview mirror, I saw her step off the porch to get a better look. She must have recognized me. I am glad she may have seen me to know I was ok; however, I am sure if she saw me, she would be more confused and upset with me.

I returned to the control center. Command walked in the room before I could take a seat.

"Gray, we have told you to forget about your past. Your past only makes you vulnerable," he said to me. I thought to myself, how did he know what I had done or was thinking? I am quite sure I watched my surroundings, and nobody was following me. They must have a tracking device on my car.

Command walked over and put a picture of an elderly Black lady on the table. She was in the hospital bandaged with a swollen eye. When I saw this picture, she immediately reminded me of Ms. Jones. I was outraged that anybody could do something like this to an elderly lady.

Then he put down another picture. It was an elderly Black man in a casket. "She was 84 years old. He was 88," Command said to me.

"There is a robbing crew terrorizing South Dekalb. They broke into the house of this elderly couple killing him and leaving her in a coma. They walked away with $100 and a couple of watches," Command said.

The rage overtook me as I looked at these pictures. Who could beat up and kill an elderly couple? This had to be the scum of the earth. Command could see the rage manifested in my face. This was the reaction they wanted from me and the reason they brought me here. He laid another picture on the table.

"This is Smoke. He is responsible; but the police cannot get anybody to come forward to testify," Command paused as he watched me fuming over these pictures.

"This is somebody's grandmother and grandfather. They will never get the chance to have Sunday dinner with them again," he said.

"We have been asked to help get justice for this family. So, do what you need to do to help this family get justice. just do not get caught doing it," Command said to me.

"There is no justice for anybody who would do this. I am not sure what I would do if I saw this person," I said to him.

"Whatever," Command stated. "Do whatever." They gave me information on where this guy normally hangs out, including his normal schedule.

I left the Control Center full of rage. I could not get the sight of that elderly couple out of my mind. I had been given everything I needed to know about this guy. I pulled up near a park off Glenwood. He was there, as they said he would be.

I parked off in the distance and watched as he and several guys were just hanging out smoking in the park. There were too many of them there at this time. Approaching them now would be too loud and messy. I will just wait.

I watched him, growing more angrier. He was just a little punk who would not ever approach anybody by himself. He was this little man with a Napoleon complex.

Smoke stayed in the park until it was dark before he headed home. Music blasted from his old school Cutlass Supreme as he drove up to his house. Getting out of his car, he approached the house.

I was dressed in black boots, black jeans, and my gray hoodie pulled over my head. I hid behind the door waiting for him to walk into the house. My heart was racing as this was my first assignment. I had done things like this before, but it was a reaction at the time. Now, I planned and plotted revenge. It just seemed different. But it was too late for second thoughts now. The door opened.

He walked in the house without noticing me, approaching the nearby table. He put the keys down on the table. He noticed the pictures on the table, he turned on the light to get a better look at them. It was pictures of the elderly couple he had beaten and robbed.

"What the F!" Smoke started to say. Before he finished, I slipped a bag over his head and tightened the zip tie around his neck. He reached for the gun in his waistband. I put my gun to the back of his head.

"Try it if you want," I said, making him stop.

"Let me get that from you," I said, taking the gun from his waist.

I led him to a chair in the kitchen, seating him in the chair. I tied his feet and hands to the chair with zip ties. I took a seat directly across from him.

"I am going to ask you a question and I want you to think carefully before you answer. You will only get one chance to answer. Do you understand?" I said to him.

He did not respond. "Just nod your head yes or no so I make sure you understand." I told him. He nodded his head, indicating he understood.

"Do you recall those pictures you saw on the table?" I said to him, and he did not respond. I took the handle of my gun and hit him across his head with the gun; knocking him to the floor.

I walked over to pick him up off the floor as he was still tied to the chair.

"Let's get an understanding. I ask questions and you answer. If you do not answer you will just piss me off. Do you understand?" I said to Smoke. Again, he did not respond. I took my gun and hit him across the head again, knocking him over.

Laying on the floor, this time he said, "I understand. Damn man what do you want?"

"Good," I said, walking over to picked him up off the ground again. "I am asking the questions here," I told him. "So, did you see the pictures on the table?"

"Yeah, I saw them," he said.

I asked him if he knew or had ever seen the people in the pictures before.

"Naw man. I ain't ever seen them people," he responded.

I stood up, and walked over to him. This time I struck him in his jaw yet again, knocking him to the floor. Again, I picked him up and sat the chair upright.

"Let's try this again. Have you seen these people before?" I asked him.

"Damn, man. What do you want?" he said to me.

"So, tell me what happened. When you robbed them, did you intend to beat them when you went there or did things just go wrong once you got there?" I asked Smoke.

"I don't know what you are talking about." Smoke said to me.

I grabbed the gun and hit him again, knocking him to the groundonce more. I walked over and picked him up.

"Let me try this another way. Are you ready to turn yourself in for killing him and beating her?" I said to him.

"Man fuck you!" Smoke yelled through the bag placed over his head.

I grabbed the gun, pulled the trigger, and shot him right between his eyes; knocking him backward this time.

"Wrong answer," I said as I got up and walked out the door.

I got back into the car and drove off. I did not think twice about anything that happened to that guy. I felt he deserved everything he got. All I could think about were the two elderly people he tortured.

I drove across town to a grocery store. I stripped off the shoes, jeans, and hoodie placing them into a garbage bag. I took the bag and threw it in the dumpster at the grocery store.

Driving to a local lake, I took the gun and threw it as far into the lake as possible.

I looked at the gun I had taken from him. It was a Glock nine. The Glock would be an ideal replacement for the gun I just threw in the lake. After following the post assignment protocol, I needed to call Command.

"Command, it's done," I said as I picked up the phone to call in the status.

"Gray, from this point forward. You cannot ever return to Control Center. You cannot ever contact me again. You will get an envelope with a cash payment of seven thousand dollars each week. When we have an assignment, we will contact you. But remember, none of this ever happened," Command said to me.

I felt accomplished as if I passed my first test.

Then Command said, "Welcome to Ghost Squad," and hung up the phone.

CHAPTER 6

LICENSE TO KILL

After Smoke, every two to three weeks I would get another assignment. With each assignment, I became less and less emotional about the job. I became desensitized, and the passion and fire that once drove me to protect the helpless was dwindling. And on top of that, I was isolated with no family and friends. If I was going to continue doing this, I was going to need to establish some sense of normalcy.

I had been following Stephanie around for quite some time, just watching over her. I felt as if I were stalking her, as I was watching her but could not approach her. She was doing rather good for herself and had opened her own beauty supply store. Her schedule was routine.

She arrived at her store at about 7:15 every morning. She was alone in the store until 8am when another employee would arrive. At 9am she would make her bank run to deposit the previous day's receipts. She worked until about 2pm when an employee would come in and work until closing. She was an easy target if anybody ever wanted to rob her.

She would go for drinks with some girlfriends every Thursday after she closed the store. She would get the same apple martini and an appetizer. She rarely ever had company at her house, except this one male that would come every so often driving a black Mercedes.

As I said, I felt like I was stalking her. It was my only way of feeling connected to her and making sure she was safe. The more I became detached from Control, the stronger my desire to reach out to her became.

As normal she arrived at about 7:15 that morning. As she was unlocking her door, I walked up behind her. I startled her and she turned and pulled a gun on me.

'Wait," I said throwing my hands up. She realized it was me and she just paused. There was an awkward moment of silence.

"Get the hell away from me," she said as she broke the silence. She unlocked the door and walked in, trying to close it on me. I grabbed the door handle before she could pull it shut.

"No, wait listen," I pleaded with her.

"Let my damn door go and go back to wherever you came from," she stated in anger.

"Please, let me come in and explain to you, I really need to explain and talk to you," I said pleading my case.

"There is nothing to explain," she said as she again tried to pull the door shut.

This exchange went back and forth. I thought she would be upset at me for everything she heard, so I was not surprised by her reaction. She finally relented, and let me in.

"I got a few minutes before my store opens; you better make it quick," she said to me with her arms crossed.

"First, I need to let you know that I did not break out of jail," I said to her.

"Stew, the damn footage of you running out of the jail was all over the news," stop lying to me.

"Well, technically I did not break out, it's complicated. Let me explain," I said to her.

"What I am about to tell you can never be repeated," I said to her making her promise not to ever repeat this conversation.

I realized the story I was about to tell her was going to be extremely hard for somebody to believe. Who would believe this cloak-and-dagger story about a mysterious, covert law enforcement group that operated outside of the law? This covert operation that was going around torturing and killing criminals all in the name of public safety.

That was going to be a hard story for me to sell to anybody. But I had to try and explain it to her to get her to believe me. This was no easy task. I was about to go against everything Command had discussed.

"You remember a few months back an old couple down the street were robbed and beaten. The husband died and the wife was left in a coma" I said trying to give her some details.

"If you recall, the police never arrested anybody. They knew who attacked them, but nobody would testify and there was not enough evidence to arrest them," I said.

"Yeah, everybody in the streets knew who did that," she said.

"Well, if you know who they think did it, then you know what happened to them," I said to her as she looked at me with this befuddled glaze in her eyes.

The more I explained, the more realistic it became to her. You could see in her eyes that she was starting to believe my story. She was starting to believe the escape was staged. She was starting to believe that the Ghost Squad really existed.

"Why has it taken you this long to contact me, and have you been watching me. I swear I felt like somebody has been watching me and I thought I saw you a few times. That is why I have this gun," she said to me.

I explained that I was told that I could not contact anybody from my past. I was told that doing so would put them and myself in jeopardy. But I was feeling so isolated and alone, I could not continue to live like that and not reach out to you. I needed a friend, somebody to confide in. Some of the things they have me doing make it hard to sleep at night.

I told her about an assignment that has continued to haunt me as I flashed back to how that one all started. Our routine was very regimented. I was to eat lunch each Tuesday and Friday at this deli. I was to be there at 11:30am each time and had to sit at the back corner table. That table allowed me to see everybody walking into the deli and close enough to the back door for an exit.

If there was an assignment, somebody would simply walk in and drop an envelope on the table. I had not heard from anybody in the program in a couple of weeks. I was there as normal enjoying a sandwich when I saw a strange individual walk in the front door.

He walked in and dropped an envelope on the table and walked out the back door. Still holding my sandwich in my hand that I had barely eaten, I stared at the envelope he dropped on the table. I put the sandwich down, pulled cash out of my pocket, and sat it on the table as I picked up the envelope and exited out the back door.

I arrived at my place and sat at the table to open the envelope. The first thing I saw was a picture of a young Black male, about 23 or 24 years old. Looked in the envelope and saw the instructions. They were usually notes that were glued on a piece of paper using letters from various magazines and newspapers.

The enclosed note said "ROBBING CREW – ELIMINATE" with pictures of the kid at various locations and the address of where I could find him. I committed the information to memory, got up and walked over to the kitchen sink. I pulled out a lighter and set the note, and the picture on fire in a pan sitting in the sink. After the documents burned, I swept the residue into the garbage disposal to grind the remains.

I went into my room, and moved the clothes in my closet to the side to reveal the hidden door in the back of the closet. I went into that hidden door, grabbed the work bag full of tools for this kind of work, grabbed some shoes, and gloves from there and walked out, adjusting the clothes back to conceal the hidden door.

As I walked out to my car and threw the bag in the trunk, I replayed the pictures and the note in my head to burn the image of this person into my memory. Being in the streets like I have been, I usually know about everything going on in the underworld, long before I was asked to do something about it.

I had not heard about this robbing crew, but if I got them sent to me, they must have done something bad to make it on my work list. It is better for me to not think about the target of my missions, just accept the assignment and execute the plan. The more I think about it the more the target becomes a person and that causes hesitation and remorse.

I arrived at his house, parked my car down the block and waited for him to arrive home. After a few minutes, he came home and drove into his garage. I watched as the garage door went down. I knew there was one other person in the house, so I was waiting for her to leave. My job is to eliminate the target, I try to never have collateral damage or witnesses.

Twenty minutes after he got home, the door opened, and a lady walked out of the house. I could see him walk her to her car as it seemed as if he kept looking around checking his surroundings. Once she pulled out of the driveway and down the block, I reached for the back seat and got my work bag.

Through his back door, I could see him sitting in a chair watching television. I got my bag and activated a cell phone jammer. That device also interrupted the wireless service, jamming any security camera video. He sat there oblivious to everything that was about to happen. I pulled out the tools and punched a hole in his deadbolt lock allowing me to unlock his door.

The houses in this neighborhood were awfully close to one another, so I needed to make this one a quiet job, this would be an up close and personal one.

I walked up behind him, and he caught a glimpse of my reflection off the television. He was not startled. He did not react at all.

"So, they sent you here after me," he said to me. I did not respond to him, and I walked closer, now on alert trying to make sure he did not reach for a gun or weapon.

"I figured somebody would be coming after me eventually. Just tell them to leave my daughter alone," he said as he got down on his knees. He began to start praying, just as I wrapped a cord around his neck. He did not resist; he continued to try and pray as he was gagging and struggling to breathe. As he was starting to black out, he reached up, and touched my arm just as he lost consciousness. He fell forward onto the coffee table and onto the floor.

I turned and walked back toward the kitchen to go back out the same door.

"Daddy," I heard a child's voice say. There was not supposed to be anybody here, especially not any kids.

"Daddy," I heard again as it seemed like the voice was coming down the stairs. I ducked behind the wall and peeked into the room. I saw a little girl come down the stairs and stand over to him.

She pushed him "Daddy, wake up! Wake up, Daddy I am hungry," she said to him shaking him. She pushed him again. Even at her youthful age, she started to realize that her dad was not sleeping.

"Daddy," I heard her say again as she started crying. She laid down on him and placed her arm around his neck. "Daddy," she cried.

I stood there and for the first time, this job had gotten to me. These were always nameless, faceless criminals that deserved what was coming. Seeing this young kid's daughter find her dad dead made this assignment different.

I backed away from the wall and out the back door as I could still hear the young girl's cry. I made my way back to my car and just sat in the car. How could I not have known there was a kid in the house? That was not supposed to happen.

I took out my burner phone.

"911, what is your emergency," the operator said.

"I think my neighbor had a stroke or something in his house, I need an ambulance," I said. I gave them the address, turned the phone off, and drove off. I went a couple of blocks and threw the phone out of the window into the woods.

I pulled up to my house and dropped my bag by the door. "Dammit," I said. I had to call 911 to make sure the little girl was ok, but why did she have to be there. I sat down at the table and felt bad about myself and that evening.

Stephanie sat there listening to the story in awe. She did not interrupt and did not say anything until I was done.

"What happened to the little girl," she said to me.

I did not answer her. I knew what happened to the girl, but did not want to say it aloud, as it would have only made me feel worse about everything.

"Well, you can see why I needed to see you. Why I needed to talk," I said to Stephanie.

"That is a lot," Stephanie said to me.

"Yes, it is. That is why I have not been able to sleep at night. I cannot get the vision of the kid hugging her dad out of my head," I told her. "I know there is nothing you can do about it, I just wanted to share it with somebody, it is not like I can tell anybody else what happened."

After I talked to Stephanie, I realized I needed to see Dr. Owens. I knew she made everything make sense when I was in jail. But could I reach out to her? I am sure she thinks I broke out of jail. I would just have to explain to her. I must meet with her.

I left Stephanie's house, determined to locate Dr. Owens. How hard would it be to locate a certified clinical psychologist that moonlighted in a federal prison? It wasn't hard and it did not take me long. I called her office and set up an appointment under a fake name.

Two days later I arrived at her office for her meeting. Her receptionist called me back and I walked into her office. She was sitting behind her desk and there was a look of shock on her face. She obviously knew I was not this James Walker person, listed on her schedule.

"Close the door," she said.

I closed the door and sat down in a chair. She walked around and sat in a chair directly across from me.

"I know you have a lot of questions," I said to her. "But first I need to make sure everything we discuss is confidential and cannot leave this room under any circumstances," I said as I looked in her face for affirmation.

I explained that I did not break out of jail. I told her all about my first meeting in jail making the offer to leave prison for the Ghost Squad. I told her about the squad and the missions that we undertake to pursue predators. I did not get into too many details. She knew of my fits of anger in jail when I targeted bullies, but I was trying to explain to her that I was no longer having these same feelings.

Working for the Ghost Squad I had become numb and apathetic. I started completing missions with no regard for human life nor thinking about the purpose of each mission. That all changed when I saw that little girl on the floor hugging and crying for her dad.

I told her I was not sure if I could continue to do this, my conscience has gotten the best of me, and I cannot continue. I told her on top of that, I saw on the news they reported the young man was a youth pastor at a church. That made me question the mission and what he meant to me when he said, "They sent you."

She was unusually quiet this time. I imagined that she was in shock about the things she had heard me say and did not know how to respond.

"Stew, what are you going to do," she finally asked me.

I did not know how to answer that question, or if I should answer that question. I poured out everything to her, letting her know my deepest thoughts. It felt good to be able to get all of that off my chest even if I thought she was not as responsive as she has been in previous sessions.

"I know my time is up, and I have to go anyway," I said to her as I stood up. "Thank you for listening," as I walked out. It was 11am so I had 30 minutes to get to the deli for lunch. I rushed out of her office and headed to the restaurant.

When I left, she made a phone call.

"Hey Latoya," the voice said.

"Marcus, he just left my office. He is cracking," she said into the phone.

"You referring to Gray," he responded.

"Yes, he is having doubts," she reiterated.

"Thank you, I will handle it," the voice said.

Back at the restaurant, I was sitting there when somebody walked in and dropped an envelope on my table. I stopped eating and dropped thirty dollars cash on the table, took the envelope, and walked out of the back door myself.

I got back to the house and opened the envelope as usual. I pulled out the picture, this time it was not some young-looking thug. This was a picture of a thirty-something-year-old Black male that did not look like he was involved in the streets. He looked like he was a person that could be me.

That made me think about how decent people could get caught up in bad situations. What could he have gotten himself caught up in that would warrant him getting sent to me with a note that said, "Terminate at the park."

I memorized everything about him, tore up his picture and the note, and burned it as usual. Went to my closet to get my gear to head out and stake out this guy. As usual, the surveillance information was exactly as stated as I had eyes on him within 15 minutes.

He arrived and I saw him getting out of the car. Then the back door opened, and two kids got out of the back seat. Looked like twin boys about 6 or 7 years old. Nobody said anything about any kids being here. Now I am sitting here watching this man, and his two boys as they got out of the car. They went and sat on a bench eating ice cream together.

Seeing him as a father struck a chord with my sensitive side. I sat and watched them eat ice cream, laugh, and play with each other. Made me realize that was something I have never experienced. I do not have any kids of my own. Any kids to take to the park to sit and eat ice cream with.

Any kids to watch them grow up and look up to me for guidance and as their role model. I sat there and visualized myself getting out of the car while he was sitting on the bench. Walking across the parking lot as he was not conscious of me being there and what was about to happen.

I would sneak up behind him and could hear his conversation and his little boys laughing as they were eating the ice cream. I got close enough to see the difference in the little boys as one of the twins had a mole on his right cheek and the other did not.

This job was to be completed quietly in public as his trip to the park was one of his most vulnerable times. I reached into my pocket and pulled out the syringe as I approached. The kids were about five feet away sitting in the dirt as their dad looked on.

I walked up, put my hand on one side of his head and jabbed the syringe full of botulinum into his neck, and walked away. He looked back at me as I walked away. You could see him grabbing his neck where I injected the poison. Then you could see him gasping for air as he started turning colors. He began foaming at the mouth unable to breathe before falling over on the bench.

I saw one of the boys look back and see their dad laying on the bench. The little boy with the mole on his cheek got up and walked over to his dad and stood there looking at him. The other twin then noticed, and he got up and walked over to join his brother.

Here are the two little boys standing there in the park looking over the lifeless body of their father as I sat in the car and watched them.

Then, I snapped out of it. I could not do that. I was not about to kill this man in front of his two little boys. I know the job was to get him at this location and this time, but I could not see myself getting out of this car and doing that today.

I started up my car and as I did, I could see him turn around to look in the direction of the car. I immediately cut my eyes to not make eye contact with him. That showed a vulnerability within me. I was scared to make eye contact with this man because I feared it would make him a human, a dad, a husband, and not some scum of the earth I was sent to eliminate.

I pulled off and out of the parking lot, as this man had no idea how close he had just come to death. As I was at the red light waiting to turn, I saw him get up and go sit on the ground with his little boys.

I saw one of them get up and hug him as he sat down. As the kid that stood up was hugging him, he put his arm around the other kid. I was watching this loving father sitting in the park hugging his two little boys as they all enjoyed ice cream together.

Then I heard a horn, behind me. Watching them and not paying attention, I did not realize the light had turned green. I hit the gas making that left turn, driving away from the park, but the thought of the two boys standing over their father's body could not escape my mind.

It drummed up the memories of the little girl. that little girl standing there. "Daddy" I heard her say again. "Daddy wake up" I heard in the little girl's voice. I was sweating and in a panic. I drove right over to Dr. Owens' office. I did not have an appointment, I just needed to see her immediately.

I walked into her office, "I need to see Dr. Owens" I said to the receptionist.

"Do you have an appointment sir," she said to me.

"No, I do not have an appointment, but I need to see her. It is an emergency," I told the lady behind the desk.

"I am sorry sir, she has a full calendar today, I can make you an appointment."

Completely frustrated and feeling like I was losing it. I slammed my fist against the counter and yelled "I need to see her now!" When I yelled, everybody in the office stopped what they were doing and turned to look at me.

You saw the door to her office open as she came out to see what the commotion was. She saw me as she opened the door. "Dr. Owens I told him you had a full schedule today," the receptionist said to her.

"That is ok, Kim. You can let him come in. He seems like he needs it," she said to the receptionist. I walked into her office and sat down. I immediately broke down near tears.

"It was happening again. I cannot stop seeing the little girl, and today I had an incident involving some little boys." I said to her trying to get this off my chest. Trying to understand why I am not having all these bouts with my conscious. Why is this job becoming harder and harder for me to do? I feel like I have seen the last couple of people as only regular citizens, I am losing it. I needed Dr. Owens to help me overcome this sudden issue.

After spending a few minutes with Dr. Owens, she was able to calm my nerves a bit. I was able to gather myself and my thoughts.

"Thank you, Dr. Owens, I just needed to get that off my chest," I said to her as I walked out.

I was walking out of the office, and I turned around and walked back to the receptionist's desk. Saw a stack of business cards on the desk and picked up the one that read 'Kimberly LeBeau.'

"Kimberly, that is your name correct?" I said to her. She nodded to me. "I am so sorry about earlier. I was just going through a lot and really needed to speak to her. I cannot talk to anybody else," I tried to explain.

"I got your card," as I held it up. "I owe you lunch or something for yelling at you," I said as I put the card in my pocket and walked out of the office.

Dr. Owens picked up the phone after I left. "Marcus, he is done," she said when the man answered.

"He just left your office," the man questioned.

"Yes, talking about these visions he can't escape," she told him.

He hung up the phone and Dr. Owens went on about her day calling the next patient into her office.

I was driving and my phone rang. I picked up the phone and saw it was a number I did not recognize. Nobody calls this phone, except for Command. I was not about to answer the phone to talk to Command right now.

I could not answer the phone. I could not tell them I did not complete the mission. I had never had to tell them that before and would not know how to break that news. I just let the phone ring until they hung up. I knew I was going to have to eventually talk to Command, and let them know what happened if they did not already know.

I was not going to go home, I wanted to drive to the lake and just sit and look out over the water. I went to buy a blanket and a remote-controlled boat to take to the lake with me. I realized it was already noon and I wanted to eat. I was not too far from the office, so I figured I would call and ask the receptionist about that lunch. I was hoping she had not already left, as there was nothing on here but an office number.

"Hello, Dr. Owens' office, how may I help you," the voice on the other end answered. I immediately recognized the voice.

"Is this Kimberly," I asked knowing what the answer would be.

"I want to again apologize for my actions today," I said to her. "I am still in the area about to eat lunch. Wanted to see if you were free to join me. As my apology," I said hoping to get a yes from her.

She laughed. "You know I am not supposed to mingle with patients right," she said to me.

"Well, I am not asking you to mingle or anything, just giving you lunch to apologize for my actions," I told her.

"I normally do not leave the office for lunch," she said to me. I was disappointed to hear that.

"But today is my half day. I get off right now actually and I could meet you. But it is just for an apology," she said to me. I told her where to meet and drove there to meet her.

I really had not had a romantic interest since I had gotten back because my job just did not allow for it mentally. And who would want to put a woman through anything that I was doing on my job? How could you even explain my job to somebody and have them believe it?

But I was sitting at the table when she walked in to join me. I could tell when she walked in the door, she had an interest in me more than just coming to get an apology lunch. The feeling was mutual. We sat there and talked for a while.

It was a good lunch and something different for me. I paid for the lunch, and we were walking out the door when she told me she needed to call a rideshare.

"I put my car in the shop this morning, so I am getting a rideshare home," she told me.

"You don't have to do that; I can take you home," I said to her. After saying no, I insisted to her that I take her home and she finally relented. We walked to my car, and I opened the door and put the boat in the back seat so she could get in.

"A remote-controlled boat," she questioned as I got in the car.

"Yeah, I felt like I needed to go to the lake today and relax, so I bought the boat to enjoy on the lake," I told her. She responded by telling me how she loved the water, and it helped her relax also.

"Well, why don't you come with me," I asked her. She paused and just looked.

"Why not, I do not have anything else to do," she said.

"Great, it would be fun" I said to her. We were pulling off and the phone rang again. I looked at it and it was another unidentified number. I definitely could not answer the phone this time and talk to Command with somebody else in the car. I looked at the phone and then at her.

"You need to answer that" she asked.

"No, it is work and I do not want to talk to them right now," I said to her as I hit the decline button on the phone.

We drove to the lake and were just enjoying the time in the sun looking out over the water. As we were sitting there on the blanket, the phone rang again. It was again an unidentified number. I was going to have to eventually talk to Command, I could not keep avoiding the call.

She looked at me. "You need to take that," she said referring to the call.

"Yeah, I do. It is work again and they are probably going to keep calling," I said.

"Excuse me one second" as I got up to walk away from her to take the call.

I answered the call "Gray, you did not perform your job this morning" I heard coming from the phone. I had not thought about how I would respond nor tell Command about today yet, so I just held the phone.

"Make sure you understand this Gray. You knew the terms when you took this job. You knew the consequences of not performing your job. So, you need to get your shit together and go and finish this job" he said to me.

I still did not respond, did not say a word. "Gray, are you there," he said to me.

"Yes, I am here," I finally responded.

"Get your head out of your ass, stop worrying about little kids, and do your damn job or else," and he hung up the phone.

I just looked at the phone. I knew the conversation was coming, just did not know how I would feel or react when it happened.

I turned to look back at Kim laying on the blanket looking up at the sky. I put the phone in my pocket and walked back over to her and laid down next to her to observe the skies also.

"You see that white goose there," I said pointing to a bird in the sky above. "He looks so majestic, so pure and innocent. That is how I want to live life" I said to her.

Then I pointed to an eagle much higher in the sky soaring with his wings spread wide. "But you see that eagle way up there. That is how I live. Out of sight in the distance. Like that eagle looking down on others with a license to kill" I said.

She turned and looked at me. "What do you mean," she said.

"Nothing, just talking about the eagle being the apex predator of the skies," I said to her.

"A license to kill everything in the air."

CHAPTER 7

TRIP TO THE DOCTOR'S OFFICE

The trip to the lake was a much-needed mental break for me. It was even better to be there with Kimberly enjoying the moment. We just enjoyed the sun, the water, laughed, and got my mind off the current situation with Ghost Squad.

As the day on the lake ended, my mind shifted to the dilemma I face upon my return. When this first started, things felt different for me. I felt I was doing things that would help to improve the community. I felt like I was an asset to society for once in my life.

I sat at the lake and watched a family out there. I watched as the dad was teaching his young boys how to fish. All of them wore bright neon green t-shirts with white shorts. On the front, it said *"Jones' Family Birthday Trip"* in yellow letters on each shirt. On the back of the man's shirt, it said *"30th Birthday Boy"*. The two little boys' shirts read, *"Dad's*

Birthday Party Crew" in big bold letters. On the back of the ladies' shirt, it read, *"It's Hubby's Birthday."*

I could not stop focusing on this man and those shirts. Every time I looked at his face, I had a flashback. I saw a vision of a mission I executed on a man's 30th birthday. I saw a bullet hole in his head with blood running down the bridge of his nose. I saw that man lying on the ground with his eyes open looking back at me. I glanced back to see the sun reflecting off the face of his watch as I walked away with him lying there by the passenger door of his car in his driveway.

I recalled a lady walking out of the house as everything seemed to be in slow motion. I heard her screams as she ran to the car, to his side. She fell to her knees beside him screaming at the top of her lungs. "help." She was oblivious to anything going on around her, as you could hear the pain in her cry from losing a man she loved.

I turned my head and kept walking away. Her screams became fainter with each step I took. I turned the block and kept walking until I could no longer hear her screams. I learned the lesson that day to never look back. In this world, when you look back you only see the carnage you have created. You only see the tears you have caused. You only see the families you have ruined. You can never look back.

Then I recalled that man in the driveway was another one of my assignments, I conducted without questioning the mission. I knew nothing about why he was one of my targets. For all I knew, he could have been an innocent man who stepped on the wrong person's shoes and was executed for doing so.

The man on the lake could have been the guy laying in the driveway. Those two boys could have been the dead man's kids who never had a chance for their dad to take them to the lake to learn how to fish.

I was not sure anymore if I was the one helping the community or the one being a detriment to the community. I was acting as the judge, jury, and execution for young Black men who never got a chance to tell their side of the story. They never got a chance to prove their innocence.

I was not sure if my inner conflicts were real, or if my conscious had reached a tipping point. The trip to the lake was therapeutic in that I was able to just get away to relax. But it also created more questions about the work I was doing, and whether I could continue down this path.

"What is on your mind? You've been awfully quiet on the ride," Kim said, breaking the silence on the ride home from the lake.

"I am sorry. A lot of work stuff was on my mind," I responded to her, not being able to go into too many details. I looked at her and smiled.

"Why are you smiling?"

I did not know how to answer that question. Yes, I liked her. The smile was about the possibility of getting to know her. Ghost Squad had made having a personal life impossible. I drove thinking about being able to sleep at night with a woman next to me.

I made it back to her house and we pulled up in the driveway. I did not want the night to end, but I did not want to rush things with her. Did not want to give her any second thoughts about my motives and what I wanted from her.

I got out of the car, walked around, and opened her door to let her out. We walked up to her front door as she fumbled through her purse trying to find her keys. She pulled her keys out of her purse and unlocked the door.

Before she opened the door, I reached down and grabbed her hand. She turned and looked at her hand and then looked up at me. I reached and grabbed her other hand as I looked into her eyes. I could see the sparkle in her eyes letting me know that she was enjoying this moment as much as I was.

"There are a lot of things in my life and in my past that I want to share with you when the time is right," I said, looking her squarely in the eyes. "My life is complicated. Spending time with you today was soothing, relaxing, and much-needed. Your spirit feels like it is everything that I needed. I don't know where this will go, if it goes anywhere, but I know at this moment you seem like the perfect woman for me."

I leaned in and gently kissed her on the jaw. "I can't wait to see you again," I said as I watched her go into her house. I stood there as the door closed and she locked it. I walked back to my car and sat down, feeling human again for the first time in a long time. Feeling like a person with real emotions.

I looked up at her door and could see her silhouette through the door. She was leaning back against the door. She was standing there with a smile on her face on the other side of the door, having the same thoughts. Seeing her standing there, let me know that the things I was feeling were mutual.

The next few weeks, I started spending more time with her. The more time I spent with her, the harder it became to emotionally continue with Ghost Squad. Each assignment became harder and harder to conduct emotionally.

After each assignment, I would rush to see Kim to regain a sense of humanity. It was like she was my calming force. She could tell that I was carrying a burden, but she would never press the issue with me. She knew that when the time was right, I would tell her everything.

She would often discuss the kids in the group she often volunteered for. She would always talk about how the kids were her peace and being around them made her appreciative of the things in life. She often talked about this little girl named Rayna whom she had taken to, and felt bad for the things life had dealt her at a young age.

"Stew, we are taking the kids to the game room this Saturday. You should come," she said to me. "It would probably be as mentally fulfilling to you as it is to me to be around them," she continued. I thought it would be a great idea to go. I would never pass up an opportunity to spend more time with her.

Saturday morning came and I had an assignment to complete prior to the event. I wanted to get this done before I rushed to see Kim and the kids she volunteers with. I knew of this guy who was the target, and he was indeed a problem in the community. I also knew of his reputation. I knew that I needed to make sure I was on point and made no mistakes. He had a reputation as a cold-blooded killer.

He always went to the gym on Saturday mornings before the sun came up. This was the time to catch him off guard. I was standing in the dark around the building watching as he got out of his car and approached the front door of the gym.

I walked from behind the building, and slowly walked up behind him. As I approached, I pulled out the knife from my pants, holding it down by my side as he got closer to the gym door. He was reaching for the key card to unlock the door when a car drove by.

As the headlights from the car went by, he could see my shadow on the building as I walked up behind him. He saw the shadow with a knife in its hands just steps away. He suddenly turned, and in one motion, fired a shot; missing me.

Scrambling for cover, I dove behind his car as I heard the second shot being fired. This one hit me on my right arm just as I got behind the rear bumper of his car.

"Who the fuck are you? Didn't anybody ever tell you not to bring a knife to a gunfight," he said as he started calmly walking towards the car. I could see his shadow from the exterior light of the building as he approached. His shadow is getting larger and larger.

I only had a knife, and he shot me in the arm. I looked around to see my quickest escape route because I knew I was hurt and could not beat a man holding a gun. I knew if he got close to me, he would shoot to kill without hesitation. He has done it before for much less.

I gathered myself and looked over toward the corner of the building from where I came. I snuck around to the other side of the car as he approached, and then I made a beeline for the corner of the building. He saw me take off running, and he turned and shot. He missed, but I could see the bullet hitting the brick on the building as I sprinted to the corner.

"No, don't run now bitch. You wanted me, come back, and get it," he said, firing another shot after I was safely around the corner of the building. After I got to the corner of the building, I sprinted toward the concrete wall at the back of the building. I jumped on the top of the dumpster and then over the top of the concrete wall.

I heard another shot; you could hear the metal on metal as the bullet hit the dumpster I had just used to hurdle the wall. After jumping over the wall, I landed, dropping my knife. It was dark, so it made it tough to find it quickly.

I could hear his footsteps as he was now running and approaching the wall. I could hear him jump on top of the dumpster to hurdle the wall like I did. I looked at the distance down this alley and knew I was not going to make it down the alley before he cleared this wall. I would have been an easy target sprinting down the alley.

I was going to have to take him head-on as soon as he cleared that wall, so I slid back against the concrete wall. I heard his feet clear the dumpster and over the wall. As he landed on the ground, I rushed in tackling him before he could safely land.

He fell to the ground, and I heard the gun sliding across the concrete alley. My momentum tackling him sent us both tumbling to the ground. I was on top of him and punched him in the face. I put my hands around his neck and began to choke him. He reached for my hands trying to pry them from his neck.

He could not break my grip. Then he took his right fist and punched me in my arm. Punching me in the same spot he had previously shot me. That loosened my grip. The pain from the punch in the arm, rattled me enough that he was able to knock me off him. I landed on the concrete pad.

He rolled over punching me in the stomach before I could move. He got to his feet and kicked me in the stomach as I lay there.

"You know you fucked up coming for me," he said as I lay on the ground agonizing in pain. He kicked me again knocking me backwards.

"I am going to cut off your head and send it back to whoever sent you," he said as he drew back to kick me yet again in the stomach, knocking me back against the building wall this time. When he kicked me this time, we both saw the gun just feet from my head.

He took a step toward the gun to grab it. I knew if he got to the gun, he would kill me on the spot. I reached up and punched him as hard as I could right between his legs. My punch doubled him over, just enough for me to regain my composure. I rolled over and grabbed both of his feet knocking him to the ground. As he fell, I climbed up to try and punch him again, he caught my arm and rolled us both over.

He was back on top of me. Then I saw him reaching for the gun. I grabbed his arm as he was reaching for the gun. I was holding his wrist trying to keep him from pointing the gun in my direction. I could see the barrel of the gun slowly turning toward me, he shot me in my arm, and I did not have much strength in it. The gun was almost pointing at my head and just a little further and he would be able to pull the trigger and shoot me in the head.

When he grabbed me and rolled us over on the ground, I felt it. I felt the handle of the knife on the ground right by my right forearm. As I was holding his wrist with my bloody and weakened left arm, I was able to feel for the knife with my right hand. Feeling around on the ground trying to see where I felt the handle.

Then, in one quick motion, I came up with the knife stabbing him in the side of his neck. He dropped the gun and immediately grabbed the side of his neck and blood started squirting out of his neck. He was losing blood so fast you could see life leaving his body.

He fell to the ground. I lay there looking at him holding his neck trying to stop the blood. The blood puddle on the concrete was getting larger by the second and his eyes were slowly closing. He was fighting to stay alive. Then he dropped his hands from the wound on his neck. His eyes closed, and his body went limp.

I just lay there for a second in pain trying to catch my breath. I looked at him lying there dead and realized that it could have been me this time. I got up, grabbed the knife and anything else I thought could link me to this place. Then I slowly walked down that alley towards my car as the morning sun was starting to rise.

I agonized in pain from the wound to my arm as I got into the car. I looked at it and saw the bullet went through the edge of my arm taking out a chunk of meat from my arm. I reached into the back of the car and grabbed rubbing alcohol and poured it over the open wound.

I grabbed the steering wheel, clenched it tight, and moaned in pain. The alcohol sent pain shooting down my body as it contacted the bullet wound. I took the gauze and covered the wound. I grabbed tape out of the medical kit and tapped the gauze in place, tearing the tape with my teeth since I only could use one hand.

I took wipes and cleaned the blood from the rest of my arm. I backed the car out of the space and turned to drive home. As I passed the alley, I turned to look and saw his lifeless body in the alley. I continued home as I had a couple of hours to get myself together before I met Kim.

I got myself together and got dressed to head out to the game room to meet Kim and the kids. I had my arm in a sling and my ribs were hurting from getting kicked in them, but I was not going to miss this opportunity to be with her and the kids doing something she enjoyed.

When I pulled up to the place, I immediately saw her standing by the door. I got out of the car and walked up giving her a hug with my one good arm.

"What happened to you?" she asked me.

"I had to do something for work this morning and hurt it. No big deal," I said to her downplaying the fact that I actually got shot in my arm just hours earlier.

"Well, I would ask you to help me carry this stuff in here, but obviously you are in no shape to do that," she said in a joking manner.

"Here, give me that bag. I can still carry it," I said, grabbing the bag from the sidewalk. We walked in and I sat the bag down in the meeting room she was setting up. I dropped some things out of the bag. I bent down and was putting those things in the bag when I saw a little girl's shoes walking up behind me.

"Hey Ms. Kim," I heard the voice say. That sound immediately caught my attention. I turned and saw Kim hugging a little girl. I could only see the red barrettes in her hair holding the two ponytails in place while they were hugging.

She let Kim go and I saw the little girl's face. I could not believe what I was seeing. My heart stopped and I froze up.

"Daddy wake up. Wake up daddy. I am hungry," I heard playing in my head. My mind was running with the thoughts of the little girl walking down the stairs shaking her dead dad telling him to wake up.

The sounds of the little girl starting to cry as she began to realize that her dad was not sleeping, and he was never going to wake up again. The sounds of that little girl's voice saying those words. The sounds of her crying. The vision of her shaking him. All things that have haunted me ever since that day.

Now, that little girl is standing in front of me again, this time hugging Kim. I could not move. I was just staring at her. I heard Kim say something, but I was in my own world looking at this little girl again.

"Stew," I heard Kim say again.

"What is wrong? Why are you looking at her like that?" she asked me.

"No reason. She just reminded me of somebody," I said trying to think of a quick response. I could not just respond, I killed her daddy and was standing there when she found him.

"Here Rayna. Here is a game card. You can go and play until it is time to come in here," she said to her, handing her a card.

"Oh Rayna, this is Mr. Stew," she said introducing her to me. The little girl turned and looked at me. For the first time. Would she recognize me? Know that I was the one who was there that day when her dad was murdered ?She looked at me with pretty brown eyes.

"Hey Mr. Stew," she said so politely, in the same voice that has been haunting me.

She turned and ran out of the room into the game room.

"Don't run Rayna," Kim said to her as she was going out the door.

"Yes ma'am," she said as she stopped running and walked around the corner. I turned and looked at Kim.

"That is the kid you have been talking about?" I asked her.

"Yes, I feel so bad for her," she answered.

"Why?" I asked.

She went on to explain to me that her mother died at an incredibly young age of cancer. "Not but a couple of months after her mom died, her dad was killed," she said to me. I already knew about the dad of course, but acted surprise to hear it.

"That is sad. What happened to the dad?" I asked her curious to hear what the rumors may be. What were people saying about her dad's death?

"I don't know. There are a lot of rumors and speculation about her dad," she said to me. It was sort of a relief to hear her say that. I always wondered, was he really into something bad or did I take out an innocent person?

"Oh, so he was in the streets and got mixed up in some stuff," I said to her, feeling better about the situation.

"Oh no. Not at all," she responded. That was not anything I wanted to hear. Was she about to confirm my thoughts that I killed an innocent person? I was afraid to ask her anything else because I was afraid of what the answer would be.

"Her dad was a youth minister," she said, and my heart sank. I killed a youth minister? Why would they have me kill a youth minister?

"He was a rising community activist who was doing a lot in the community to stop violence," she said to me. My heart started racing, hearing her say he was doing things in the community to stop violence; yet, I was told to kill him because of the violence he was responsible for.

"Rumor is that he had some information on some dirty cops who were killing people in the hood. He got too close, and they killed him," she said. I froze. She confirmed things I had started to fear. I was no longer hunting down violent criminals, I was doing the work of violent criminals.

Her words gave me this sick feeling in the pit of my stomach. Could what she said be true? If so, how could I have been so gullible to not see it before now? What was the point of it all? I just stood there in complete shock.

"So, what is up with the little girl now?" I asked trying to take my mind off those thoughts.

"She stays with her grandmother. Unfortunately, she is sick and in the initial stages of dementia, so we do not know what will happen to her. She does not have any other family, and the state is going to take her from the grandmother soon. So, we do all we can with her for now," Kim continued.

Of all the places and people on earth, I had come face to face with the little girl who has been haunting my dreams and giving me sleepless nights. The two women I think about at night, for different reasons, by some random fates are connected with each other.

This is making me sick to my stomach. I walked out to the game room area looking for this little girl. I saw her standing watching other kids on a video game. I just watched her, thinking about the things I had done that had ruined her life. The innocent victims I had once championed for, I was the one causing their pain.

It almost brought me to tears as I watched her and those two little ponytails. Just enjoying life, not knowing the man who was responsible for the death of her father was standing just feet away from her. The sickness I felt deep inside could not be explained.

I walked over to where she was standing. "Hey Mr. Stew," she said in her innocent voice. The same voice that haunts me at night.

"Rayna, you want to play a game?" I said to her, pointing to the race car game beside her.

"Sure," she said with excitement in her voice.

I helped her into the seat of the car and paid for her game. I sat in the car next to her, paid for mine, and we were set to race against one another. I could hear the excitement as screams in her voice as she was navigating the turns and jumps in the game. I watched her more than driving my own car.

"I won!" she said in excitement as the game ended. I looked up at the screen, indeed she did win.

"Can we do it again?" she said.

"Sure," I responded as I swiped the game card again to start another race. I just watched her again as we raced, thinking about all the things that had been taken from her. Thinking about how she could never do this with her daddy because I robbed her of that chance.

She dragged me all over the game room for the rest of the evening, playing one video game after another. I had become her new best friend. It gave me a sense of joy to be able to put a smile on her face; even though I carried a dark secret.

The event ended, and I walked Kim out to her car. Rayna was walking beside us because Kim was taking her back to her grandmother's house. I gave Kim a hug and turned to say goodbye to Rayna. She ran up to me and gave me a huge hug.

"Bye Mr. Stew," she said while hugging me tightly.

"Bye Rayna," I responded before getting her settled into the car. I watched them drive off and walked to my car. I sat in my car and took in everything which transpired. I began to tear up thinking about it all, and my thoughts started turning to rage.

"Stop worrying about little kids," I heard the voice of command in my head. I sat there and replayed everything in my mind. Meeting Dr. Owens in prison. What made them choose me of all the people in prison?

"Stop worrying about little kids," again echoed in my head. How did command know anything about me worrying about little kids? I had never discussed those nightmares with anybody except Dr. Owens. Then I thought about it. Dr. Owens saw me when I was in prison. When I went to her office that day, she did not seem surprised about the things I told her I was doing.

Not long after I told her about the dreams of the little girl, Command called to tell me to stop worrying about little kids. Dr. Owens is involved in this. It all dawned on me as I sat there in the parking lot. As I played back every stage of this in my mind, it all led back to Dr. Owens getting me involved in all of this.

It was time to take a trip to the doctor's office.

CHAPTER 8

I DECLARE WAR

I sat in the parking lot, trying to piece this all together. Who was Ghost Squad and how does Dr. Owens tie into this all? As I sat there, I became more skeptical of everything and everybody. I sat there wondering who I could trust.

It dawned on me, Kim works for Dr. Owens, is she a part of this all? Is she just here to keep an eye on me to report back? Damn, I felt like I had been played the fool and fell for it. I had no idea what to do or think. It was not as if I could turn to anybody for help, I had committed multiple murders all in the name of public safety.

I could get the electric chair if everything I had done was ever revealed to real law enforcement. Was the Ghost Squad even law enforcement? I had so many questions and not enough answers.

I left the parking lot and drove straight to Stephanie's house. I pulled up in her driveway as confused as I had ever been in life. When she opened the door, she could see it in my face.

"Stew, what have you done now," she said as soon as she saw me.

I could not fake it like everything was ok, and I obviously could not hide it from her. I walked into her house and sat down in the living room.

"Let me get me some wine, I can tell whatever is on your mind will be deep," she stated while walking into the kitchen. "You want something to drink Stew?"

"Naw, I am good," I said. She returned to the living room with her wine and sat down on the sofa.

"So go ahead and tell me what is wrong," she said as she got comfortable.

I did not even know where to start. She knew a little about Ghost Squad of course, but this was a different twist.

"First, I ran into the little girl," I said to Stephanie. Her eyes lit up, and she sat up in her chair.

"You ran into THAT little girl, and how did that happen?" she said eagerly awaiting a response.

"That is the problem" I led off telling her. I had to backtrack and tell her about Kim and how I met her. Told her about the doctor's office and our first day at the lake. Told her about the time we spent together and how I was feeling about her.

"Sounds like you really like her, when do I get a chance to meet her," Stephanie said.

"See, that is where this all gets complicated," I responded to her.

Stephanie sat back in her chair and took a sip of her wine. Crossed her legs and said "Boy, what is complicated about you liking somebody. It is way overdue."

"Let me finish," I responded. I reminded her of the sequence of events that led to me obviously breaking out of jail and joining Ghost Squad. I told her about how I had begun to question the assignments I was being given. How I had doubts that I was serving on the side of good.

I told her how Command had virtually threatened me and how Command knew about my struggles thinking about the little girl."

"Command knew this, but the only people I ever told were you and Dr. Owens," I said to her.

Stephanie sat back up in her chair again. "So, you think your doctor is working with the group and she identified you from prison," she questioned.

"I believe so," I responded to her.

"Oh, so now I get it. You think your new female friend may be in on this too," she said as she sat back in her chair again.

"Exactly," I told her. She could be in on this and did not know if I could trust her. I felt getting emotionally attached to somebody had become the liability that Command had preached it would be.

Stephanie let me vent and think this all through. It gave me time to process and think about what I should do next. "Steph, I got to go. I am going to get answers," I said to her as I got up and headed toward the door.

I knew exactly where Dr. Owens lived. It was a Saturday afternoon, and I am sure she was in her backyard as usual. She sat there with a drink in her hand. She looked as if she saw a ghost when she saw me standing in her yard. The look on her face was not one of seeing a friend or a patient. It was one of fear.

"Are you in on it," I said as I walked towards her.

"In on what", she responded to me.

"Don't fucking play with me. Are you in on it? You are the reason. You have ruined my life," I said to her as I was now standing arm's length away from her. You could see her hand shaking with fear. Her face changed colors and her voice trembled as she tried to speak.

"You had me killing innocent people," I said as I stood over her.

She reached out towards the table to try and grab her purse. I grabbed her hand before she got her purse.

"Don't even think about it," I said as I let her hand go and picked up the purse. I opened it to see a silver handgun tucked away inside. I took the gun out of the purse and threw it into her swimming pool. I picked her up by her neck and carried her over to the pool.

You could see the tears running down her face. Her feet were dangling in the air as I walked over to the pool carrying her with my arms around her throat. I laid her down on her stomach on the edge of the pool.

"Where does Command live?" I said to her.

"I don't know," she said.

I grabbed her by the back of her head and pushed her face under the water. She was reaching and trying to grab my hand. She was kicking and squirming as she was trying to break free from my grasp.

I pulled her up out of the water. She was breathing hard, crying, and choking on the water in her lungs. She was pleading with me to stop and let her go.

"Where does Command live," I asked her a second time.

"I don't know," she repeated her initial response. Again, I pushed her face underwater and held her down. She was kicking and fighting for her life. She kicked her shoes off as she was kicking so hard.

I pulled her back up. Fluids running from her nose. She was crying. She was begging for mercy.

"I promise, I don't know," she said between breaths. "He just calls me, or I just call him. I have only seen him once in my life. He just told me to identify people that would be a good psychological fit for a new department he was leading. I never knew it would turn into what it has."

"No don't," she said as she saw the look on my face as I was about to push her underwater again. She was panicking and flailing for dear life with her head underwater.

I let her up and walked away. She rolled over coughing and crying. She balled up in the fetal position by her pool crying as I walked out of her backyard. I partially believed her story. She may not have known initially what they were doing, but I am sure she is aware now. Though she deserved to die right there, I walked away and let her live.

"And you can call him and tell him I quit, and I am coming for him," I said as I disappeared around her house. There was no turning back at this point. I had drawn first blood and started a war with Ghost Squad that was not going to stop until the casket dropped on one of us.

It did not take long for me to turn the corner before she ran into the house and grabbed another gun. I saw her looking out of the window watching me pull off. She picked up her phone and made the call.

"He just tried to kill me," she cried into the phone.

"He was at your house," the voice said from the other end.

"Yes, I just said he tried to kill me in my own backyard. He is out of control," she said still crying.

"You might want to pack your things and find somewhere else to stay for a while," he told her. "We will take care of it," as he hung up the phone.

I had to make another stop. I needed to know who was on my side and who was not. I drove to Kim's house. I pulled up in her driveway and put my gun in my waist just in case it was needed. She came to the door and was surprised to see me there.

"Hey, I didn't know you were coming by," she said to me with a smile on her face. She could see the look in my eyes that this was not a pleasant visit.

"Are you involved," I said as I walked in her door. She took a step back as her face turned from a smile to one of concern.

"Involved in what, what is wrong with you," she said as she was backing away from me.

"Are you fucking involved," I said as I continued to walk toward her.

"What are you talking about," she said as she continued to back up until she was up against the wall.

I slammed my hands against the wall on both sides of her head preventing her from moving. "Are you involved with Dr. Owens and Ghost Squad? Do you know what they are doing?" I yelled in her face.

She began to cry in fear. "You are scaring me. I do not know what you are talking about."

"Did Dr. Owens put you up to it," I said with restraint, as I did not want to touch her.

"What are you talking about," she said. "She does not even know we talk; I could lose my job."

"You are saying she does not even know you have been seeing me outside of the office," I said to her confused and concerned. I was threatening this woman I was growing to love thinking she was betraying me, and I could be wrong.

"Dammit," I said as I turned away from her and walked away a few steps.

She reached and grabbed a knife from a nearby table. "Get the hell out of my house," she said wielding this knife.

"No," I said raising my hands up to show her I was not being a threat. "Please let me explain, I am sorry I don't know what is going on and who is in on it," I said to her backing out of the reach of her knife.

"Get the hell out," she shouted taking another step toward me.

"Please, put the knife down," I pleaded. "Let me explain."

"Ain't shit to explain, you won't get another chance to put your hands on me," she stated.

"Listen, your boss is a murderer, and she has put my life in danger. I did not know if you were involved too," I told her. That caught her attention as she lowered the knife.

"Let me just get that from you and I will explain," I said reaching for the knife and taking it out of her hand.

"I am so sorry," I started with. I sat her down and explained it all to her. I told her about Ghost Squad and her boss identifying me in jail. I told her that they were not just killing criminals. They were targeting innocent people. I told her everything, except about Rayna's dad. I could not bring myself to tell her I did that.

She sat there with an incredulous look on her face and did not speak for a moment.

"I told you there were rumors about something like this, I told you that is why they said Rayna's dad was killed," she said to me.

I looked away in shame when she said that. I did not have the heart to look her in the eyes.

"Do you know anything about her father," she asked me.

I turned and looked at her. "What you were thinking is probably true, that is probably why they targeted him. He was going to tell. That is why they are now going to try and kill me." I told her.

"I am sorry, I am so sorry. I must go before I get you involved in this," I said as I got up and walked toward the door.

As I walked out of the door, I turned and said, "Do not mention any of this to your boss, I have to figure it out," and I left.

I drove off thinking about what was next for me. I knew it was time for me to take Command down. Time for me to take down the whole Ghost Squad, but this was not going to be an easy task. I just needed to make sure I stayed away from Kim so that she did not get involved.

Monday morning came, and Kim headed to work with a lot on her mind. Dr. Owens came into the office, and she said, "Good Morning." Everybody spoke except for Kim, she just stared at her. "Kim, can you bring me Andre Patterson's file," Dr. Owens said as she was headed into her office.

Kim gathered the file, walked into her office, dropped the file on her desk without speaking, and walked out. Dr. Owens looked at the file hastily thrown on her desk and then looked up at Kim walking out of the office.

Later that morning Dr. Owens asked her for another file. Again, she walked in and dropped it on her desk without speaking, and turned to walk away.

"Kim, shut the door and come here please," she said to her before she could leave the office.

"Do we have a problem today?" Dr. Owens asked her. "No," she blurted back.

"If we do not have a problem today, why the attitude?"

Kim sat there thinking for a second about how she could approach this. She could not ask her about Ghost Squad and murderers. But, she was very curious to know if what was said about her boss was true.

"I am sorry Dr Owens. I just started seeing somebody and we just had a bad weekend", she said to her trying to lead into the conversation to see her reaction.

"You never told me you were dating somebody," Dr. Owens said to her.

"Well, I did not say anything because it was kind of a touchy situation, but I will tell you now. He is a patient here" she told her. She wanted to hit her with the name to see the reaction on her face.

"Really, a patient here?" she questioned.

"Yes, I started dating Derek Stewart," she said looking intently to see her boss's reaction. Dr. Owens' face turned pale. She took a deep breath. Kim saw the look in her eyes that confirmed the things I told her were true.

"Derek," she said finally speaking. "What were your issues this weekend," she said inquiring now and looking to see Kim's reaction. Looking to see what Kim knew.

"Nothing major. I don't know why I am so upset anyway. I just wanted him to take me somewhere and he said he could not because of work," she came up with to downplay the moment.

"Dr. Owens I am sorry. I should not have brought that to work with me," she said as she was walking out the door. Kim saw the look and realized that the rumors about Rayna's dad, the things I had said, were all probably true and her boss was involved.

"Shut the door, Kim," Dr. Owens said as she was picking up the phone.

"Hey, your guy has been dating my assistant," she said into the phone.

"That is useful information to know. Do not say anything to her. Just let us handle everything from here out and let us know if she leaves work for the day and I need you to tag her before she leaves," he said.

Kim tried to act normal at work, but the things she knew were too much for her to handle. She went to Dr. Owens and told her she was feeling sick and needed to take a half day. Her leaving early led her boss to believe that she knew more than she was letting on. She knew that she was not sick, and she probably knew too much about Ghost Squad, and that would be a problem.

"Sure, hope you feel better," she said to her. "Hey Kim wait. I know you love chocolate chip cookies. Here is a box somebody gave me, and I took them just for you," she told her insisting that she take the cookies.

Command told her to inform them if she left for the day, and Dr. Owens did just that. As soon as Kim walked out of the office, she picked up the phone and made the call.

"She just came in and said she was sick and took the rest of the day off," she said and hung up the phone.

Kim walked out to her car, got in, and just sat there. She began to cry, as she contemplated what she had gotten herself into. The woman she worked for and admired for so many years, engaged in some unthinkable acts in the community. The man she had grown to really care about, was somehow mixed up in all of this.

She looked around to make sure nobody was in the parking lot and made a phone call. I answered.

"Stew, she is involved. I believe you. I saw it on her face. I don't know what to do, what have I gotten myself involved with," she blurted out in a panic.

"Calm down Kim. Calm down. Where are you now," I asked her.

"I told her I was sick, and I had to leave work," she responded.

"Good, now DO NOT go home. Go to an ATM machine and get enough cash to get you a hotel room for a few nights. Pay for the room in cash, do not use any cards.

"Park your car in the back of the hotel, near the closest exit," I told her.

"And just stay there for a few days and relax. Take the next day or two off until I resolve this situation," I emphasized to her.

"Wherever you go, make sure nobody follows you. Turn off the Bluetooth and GPS on your phone and go somewhere you normally would not go if you went to a hotel. I will handle this," I assured her.

"You are scaring me," she said.

"Don't be scared, you will be fine. You just need to take some safety measures for a couple of days," I said trying to calm her.

She did what I asked. She drove across the street to the bank and took out one thousand dollars from the ATM machine. She drove across town to south Atlanta to a small town called Newnan and found a hotel. She checked into her hotel and paid cash as I told her to.

Kim spent the rest of the day nervous not knowing what to expect. I told her not to call me, I would reach out to her, so she sat in the room patiently waiting. She got hungry so she walked across the street to the gas station to get a drink and some chips.

She walked back to her hotel and got on the elevator, to go up to her sixth-floor room. As she got off the elevator, exited the elevator foyer, and as soon as she turned left to go down the hall to her room, she saw two men standing near her room dressed in all black with guns.

She saw them kick the door in and rushed into her hotel room. She panicked and caught herself as she was about to scream. She ducked into the laundry room and called me as she hid behind the door.

"Stew, somebody just kicked in my hotel room door," she could be heard whispering into the phone with fear in her voice. Her voice was trembling.

"Where were you," I said to her.

"I went to the store, and they were there when I came back. I am hiding in a laundry room right now," she said.

I told her to stay on the phone as she told me the hotel in which she was staying. I made a U-turn in the middle of the street as I headed to the interstate thinking I was at least 30 minutes from Newnan.

"Stay on the phone and don't move," I told her.

"I can hear them in the hallway" she whispered. I could hear their voices through the phone. I heard one of them say, *She drives a white Honda, let's go see if it is still in the parking lot.*

"They are right outside this door," she whispered as she could see them through the window.

"Don't speak," I told her. I could hear the ding of the elevator door.

"Did they get on the elevator," I asked.

"I think they did," she responded.

"Listen, they think you are in your car, you are still in the rental car, correct?" to which she responded that she was still driving the rental car.

"Great, take the stairs and go out the back door to your car," I stated. She reached down feeling her pants pocket and realized she had left her keys in the hotel room. I told her to make sure the hall was clear, run to the room and grab her keys.

She slowly opened the door and peeked out to make sure nobody was in the hall. Once she knew it was clear, she ran down the hall into her room. She grabbed her keys off the nightstand, grabbed her purse and the chocolate chip cookies, and ran down the back stairs.

The two guys outside looking in the front parking lot for her white Honda got a call. "She is moving," Command said, and they turned to run back into the hotel. "You take the stairs; I will get on the elevator," one of them said to the other.

He was running up the stairs to the sixth floor as she was coming down. She saw the man in all black enter the stairwell below. She immediately got off the stairs on the fourth floor and stood by the door waiting for him to run past it.

"Don't move until you hear him open the door above," I told her. She could hear the footsteps getting closer as they were running up the stairs. She stood with her back against the wall, praying he kept running to the sixth floor to her room. She could hear he had reached the landing near the fifth-floor door. And he kept running. Up another flight to the sixth floor. She heard the door open.

Then she went back out the door and ran down the five flights of stairs to her rental car parked by the exit as I told her to. She jumped in her car and drove off.

"How did they find me," she asked.

"Did you take anything from work, your computer, work phone, anything," I asked her.

"No, I did not take anything. Just grabbed my purse and left," she told me. "Wait, she did give me these cookies," as she looked at the bag of cookies.

"Check the bag," I told her. She dumped all the cookies out on the seat. And she saw it. There was an Apple air tag in the bottom of the bag.

"Dammit, throw it out the window right now," I told her. She stopped at the red light, rolled down her window, and threw it out.

"Get on the interstate and drive north," I said to her as I heard a loud crash.

I heard her scream and faintly yell, "Damn somebody hit me from behind."

"Kim, take off," I yelled into the phone with no response.

"Kim, can you hear me," I repeated. The impact from the wreck had knocked her earpiece off and on the floor. She couldn't hear me, though I could hear her.

"Drive off," I was hopelessly yelling into the phone as I heard her open the car door.

"No, do not get out of the car, drive off," I said again.

I could hear her, "Did you not see the light was red," yelling at the person that hit her. Then I heard her scream. "Let me go," I heard through the phone. I heard her yell for help as her voice became more distant.

They had grabbed her and thrown her in the back of a van. I was driving towards her with this helpless feeling. I had just listened as they kidnapped her. I had the feeling all over again of not being there to help somebody I loved.

Visions of seeing my dad at that bus stop, eyes wide open looking at me as he lay there dead from the bullet wound. I envisioned standing there as it happened and cried as I did nothing and just let it happen. I had visions of walking down the street to the site of the police cars at Old Lady Jones house. I walked through the crowd to get a better view, just in time for me to see them load Old Lady Jones' dead body into the ambulance.

Here I am again, helpless and doing nothing all over again. I began to feel that rage I had not felt in a long time. The rage that landed me in jail. The rage that landed me in the Ghost Squad. The rage I had lost, I felt it again.

I raced down the interstate to where she said she was staying. I knew they would no longer be there, but maybe I would be able to find something there, or in her room to help me figure out where they had taken her.

I got off the exit and could see the police cars near the red light. I saw the red Mustang with the driver's door open and the rear end crushed from the impact of being hit from behind. The police were standing there talking to witnesses.

As I drove past it, the sight of the wreck made me even more angry, as if that was even possible. I went to the hotel, parked my car, and ran up the stairs to her sixth-floor room. I could see the door still half open as it had been knocked off the hinges.

I walked in to see what I could find. There was nothing there, except the black slides she would always put on when she left work.

I sat down on the bed on the verge of tears. I needed to gather my thoughts and try and think about what to do next.

I sat there and got an alert from my phone. I picked it up and it was a text message from an unknown number. I clicked on the message. My heart stopped beating. I dropped to my knees on the hotel floor. Tears started running down my face as I dropped the phone.

For months I had started to believe Command was crooked and had me targeting innocent people. Had me killing people that were for reasons other than public safety. I had my suspicions and I just kept on working anyway.

I thought about the innocent lives I had changed forever. About Rayna and her entire world being turned upside down because of Command. The rage, anger, and guilt for allowing myself to be an accomplice was boiling over. Now, they had gone too far.

I picked the phone back up. There it was again. I could see the black sleeve covering a person's arm. I could see the gloves that had blood all over them. I saw the plastic tarp in the background. I saw blood frozen in time in this picture as you could see where it was dripping. The picture captured the blood droplets in the air. In this picture, I saw her face. I saw the trademark dark red lipstick she always wore. I saw her perfectly shaped eyebrows. I saw the dimple on her cheek that I always thought was so sexy. I saw a man holding Kim's decapitated head in his hand. The text message read "*We told you to never discuss Ghost Squad.*"

I closed my eyes, as I couldn't bare seeing this any longer. I had witnessed many horrific scenes before, and this time they made it personal.

Ghost Squad, I declare war.

CHAPTER 9

ROAD TO RECOVERY

I had no idea where to start. I want to kill them all after what they did to her. Dr. Owens, Command, and anybody else involved. They had crossed the line and made it personal. The fear of them possibly sending me back to jail was nothing compared to the revenge I wanted to seek.

The thoughts of Kim, Rayna, and all the innocent people that had fallen victim to this corrupt unit. Those were just the ones I knew of; I am sure there were dozens more. I needed to find out who was behind this and take it all down.

Thinking of Rayna, I forgot that today was the day that Kim normally picked Rayna up from her after-school program. I had to go there for her, part guilt from what I did to her dad and just not knowing if she would be standing there alone waiting for somebody to pick her up who was never coming.

I pulled up and saw her. She was standing on the corner with her pink backpack on. Her backpack matched the pink high-top tennis shoes she wore. Hair in two ponytails with pink barrettes on the end.

At first, she did not recognize the car. I blew my horn and rolled the window down. "Hey Rayna," I said to her as she looked in the door.

"Hey Mr. Stew. Where is Ms. Kim?" she said questioning why I was there.

"I am sorry Rayna, but she couldn't make it, so I am here for her," I told her. I could not dare break the news to her right now. I did not even know how to tell her if I wanted.

She got in the car. When she got in, she reached across the seat and hugged me around my neck. She tightly held the hug. I was taken aback by the hug. When she sat back in her seat, I could see her face. She was on the verge of tears.

"What is wrong Rayna?" I asked her. Thinking maybe somebody was bullying her at school. She didn't look at me and just said, "Grandma been really sick. They told me she died. I was hoping Ms. Kim would pick me up and I could go stay with her because I do not want to have to stay in a shelter," she said as she broke down crying.

I reached over and hugged her, as my eyes began to tear. This little girl has been through so much in life already ,and now this; all in the same weekend.

"You won't have to stay in a shelter," I assured her. She sat back in her seat and just stared out the window. She did not say anything, and this was an extremely awkward moment. I had no idea how to console a little kid.

I called Stephanie. "Hey, I need you to meet me at the lake house. I may need you to stay there for awhile," I said to her. I had rented a house on a lake where I would go to get away. Nobody knew about this house but Stephanie and Kim.

Rayna and I arrived at the lake house. She put her book bag down in the living room. I did not know what to do or say, but I know the water always calmed my nerves. I told her to follow me as I walked out the back door to the dock by the lake. We sat down on the dock looking over the water.

We could see the school of white ducks so gracefully and elegantly gliding across the water. Rayna was fascinated by the ducks.

"Are those your ducks?" she asked me.

"No, they just live around here," I told her.

"Do they have names?" she said.

I told her I did not think they had names, but she could name them if she wanted.

There were four ducks. They were swimming toward us, as she threw a piece of bread into the water.

"The first one, the big one, that is Mike," she said. "The others are: Delores, over there; Kim, right there; and the little one is Rayna," she said. I was speechless, sad, and guilt-ridden. Mike, that was her dad's name. Her grandmother's name was Delores, and of course, there was Kim.

That was this little girl's entire world, and everything was taken away from her. I was partly responsible for that. Then a much bigger duck came from behind us and got into the water. He swam off and the other four followed him.

"That duck is Stew," Rayna said. The irony that she just had me leading her and her family was not lost on me. She reached over and hugged me. I put my arm around her and held her as I watched the ducks swim away.

"Rayna, how about you stay here for a few days, and we can take you to school?" I told her.

"You and Ms. Kim?" she asked me. I was not ready to break the news to her.

"No, Ms. Kim is sick right now," I said, as that was the first thing that came to mind.

This little one who had faced so much in her life responded, "is she dead too? Everybody I love dies," she said with a straight face.

I did not know what to say. What little child her age should be having thoughts like that? About that time, Stephanie walked into the backyard. It was a good thing because I did not know how to respond to Rayna's last statement.

"Rayna, this is Ms. Stephanie. She is going to help look out for you when I am away," I told her. We all walked back into the house, and I walked her up to her room. It was a second-floor room with a window that allowed her to look out over the lake to see the ducks swimming from there.

"I got to get ready for work," I told her. She ran over to me and hugged me.

"You going to come back, aren't you? You are not going to leave me too?" she said. This little girl was pulling at my heart. Her strength through tragedies had me falling for this little one as if she was my own daughter.

Stephanie walked in and asked her if she wanted to bake some cookies. They both ran down the stairs and into the kitchen. I walked into the basement and gathered some tools. Grabbed my duffle bag and threw on my trademark gray hoodie.

Whenever I put on this hoodie, it was as if it transformed me into another person. I knew wearing this meant business. I snuck out the back door and drove off. Time to send a message.

I had spent the last couple of days researching and found out a lot about Command, and even had a name and address. I was about to take the fight to his doorstep.

I found out where the headquarters were, and I had a plan for it. I was sitting in a car outside of the headquarters, waiting on Command to arrive. I could see him park and get out of the car. As he got out of the car, a little kid ran up to him and handed him a manila envelope.

"What is this?" he said to the little boy.

"I don't know. A man just gave me one hundred dollars and told me to give it to you when you pulled up, and then leave" the boy said as he pulled off on his bike. He just looked at the envelope and then looked around to see if he noticed anybody watching. He could not see me, or the car I was in.

I reached down and grabbed the little gray device. I flipped the glass cover and pressed the red button. Then there was a loud "Boom." He looked up to see the entire roof blown off the building. He could see the flames coming from the top of the building. He saw the right side of the building, the entire wall gone. Bricks from that side dispersed all over the courtyard. The vibrations from the sound of the explosion set off car alarms all over the parking lot. You could hear dozens of car horns overriding the sound of the burning building.

Command just stood there looking at it all in shock. I would imagine he was more shocked that somebody located the headquarters; than he was that it just exploded in front of his eyes. I could see him look back down at the envelope the young boy had given him.

I saw him checking the weight before gingerly shaking it to see if there was anything moving inside. Once he felt comfortable it was not an explosive, he slowly started to open the envelope. I wish I knew what was going through his mind the moment he opened it.

I saw him pull the pictures out and just look at them. I could imagine his thoughts. He believed he lived in anonymity, and nobody knew of his identity. He believed he was untouchable. But here he was sitting in the parking lot watching as his office building burn down from the explosion, holding in his hand's pictures of his wife and two kids which I had the young boy deliver to him.

I started the car and drove off. I didn't want to kill him now. I wanted to make him suffer. I wanted to terrorize him until I got to the entire infrastructure of Ghost Squad. He knew I was in attack mode, and I was going to bring the fight to him.

I drove off and could hear fire trucks in the distance. I just smiled at the sound. He got what he deserved. I drove back to the lake house and snuck in the back door. Rayna and Stephanie were in the house watching TV and had not noticed me come in.

I saw the two of them sitting there and realized that these were the only two people in the world whom I had to live for. Stephanie because she is the sister, friend, and confidant who has been with me all the days of my life. And this little girl whom I felt I owed so much too. I felt like I had taken away her innocence and ruined any chance of a normal life. It was my obligation to restore any kind of normalcy to her life.

I stayed low for a few days after the attack on the office, as I knew the streets would be hot. I just stayed in the house, took Rayna to school, and picked her back up. I had finally broken down and told her Kim would not be coming back. She took it a lot better than I thought she would. It seemed as if she had just become immune to death and grown to expect it at such a young age.

I picked her up from school as normal, but I had a funny feeling this day. Things just seemed a little strange. I could not put my finger on it, and I did not notice anything out of the ordinary. I just had a weary feeling.

I decided I would drive in circles a little on the way home to make sure nobody was following us. Once I felt safe that we were not being followed, I turned into the subdivision to head to the lake house. As we walked in, I locked the door and turned on the alarm. I pulled the cameras up on my phone to observe everything.

I saw a car stop in front of the house near the mailbox. In the rear camera, I saw a couple of guys approaching the house from the lake. I grabbed Rayna and rushed downstairs. I took her to the safe room.

"Stay in here. Do not open this door for anybody. Whatever you do, do not come out of this room. Nobody can get in here unless you let them in," I said to her. She didn't say anything. She just looked at me as I shut her in the room. I rushed back up the stairs checking out the camera on my phone.

I could see they were near the house, about to break in from both the front and the back. I positioned myself by the front door to be able to get a clean shot at the door. Then it all started. I was being attacked by Ghost Squad.

Three guys kicked in the front door. The first guy wearing a black hoodie stepped inside the shadow of the door. I fired off a shot, striking him right in his chest. I could see the other two ducking back outside the door as he fell. They pulled him out of the doorway.

I stood there ready for them to attack. I was nervous and could see the guys in the back had trouble getting through the security door. It bought me a little time to deal with the guys in the front.

One of the guys in the front reached in the door and threw something in my direction. I saw it land and roll toward me. It was a flash bang. It exploded just a few feet away from me. The repercussion knocked me down. I could feel tingling in my ears as I had lost balance and was having trouble focusing. I couldn't see.

The force of the flash bang had me disoriented and confused. I knew I needed to get to some cover until I could gather my senses. I pulled myself around the counter and hid behind the ceramic tile island in the kitchen.

I could hear the guys in the house, as I hid in the kitchen. I slowly began to be able to see clearly. Just as my vision cleared, I could see a reflection off the stainless-steel refrigerator of a guy approaching.

As he slowly approached, I braced myself to shoot as he neared the island. As his reflection grew bigger, I raised my gun. When I thought he was close enough, I tried to get the jump on him and fired in his direction. He jumped behind the wall, firing back at me. We both missed, but the sound of the gunshots alerted the rest of them to our location. As I sat behind the island, somebody started unloading with an automatic weapon. I could see the bullets shattering the tile all around me. I knew I had to get out of that kitchen and away from the line of fire.

I reached over the counter and blindly fired one shot in the direction of the sound. Then I crawled on the floor out of the kitchen into the next room. Once I was out of the shadow of the kitchen door, I stood up and rushed around the living room.

The layout of the house was such that I could walk around and approach the kitchen from behind them. Sneaking up on them. As I turned the corner to sneak up on them, one of them was looking in my direction and started firing. I ducked for cover, as their bullets pierced the drywall just inches from my head.

The guys from the back of the house had made it to that area now. I was outnumbered, and these were highly trained individuals, much like me. There was only one way for me to end this. One last chance.

I looked, and the basement door was on the other side of the house. I had to get to the basement door. There were a couple of guys standing between me and that door. The only way I was going to make it out of here alive was to get to that door.

I picked up a lamp that was next to me. I ducked back around the wall where I left the kitchen. I threw the lamp in that direction, breaking it off the wall. The guys all heard the sound and started walking in that direction trying to corner me.

As they started walking that way, I began sneaking in the opposite direction to try and make my way to the basement door. I heard an automatic weapon unload, and I started running for the door.

I did not make it to the door before one of them saw me and turned to fire. His first shot I heard go whisking by my head. His second shot, I was not so lucky. He hit me on my side. I raised my gun to return fire.

I was only a few steps from the basement door. He fired another shot, which hit me as I reached the door. I dove through the basement door, reaching for that nondescript drawstring which always hung from the ceiling in the stairwell.

I was in mid-air and had one chance to grab the drawstring before I tumbled down a flight of stairs. The pain from the two gunshot wounds was excruciating as I reached for the handle. As I grabbed the handle, another person reached the door to the basement and fired a shot in my direction while I was mid-air.

I fell down the flight of stairs holding on to that draw string. When it was pulled, it dropped an iron door at the entrance to the basement, sealing it off. Once that lever was pulled, it made the basement a safe room, but that was just step one.

I landed on the floor some fifteen feet below. I could barely move from the pain of the bullet wounds and the fall down a flight of stairs. But I had to get back up. I had to hit the light switch. I grabbed the handrail at the bottom of the stairs.

I pulled myself up to a sitting position. I reached up, but still could not reach the light switch. I was starting to feel faint, I was losing energy and felt that I would pass out at any minute. I had to reach this light switch, or they would eventually get in here, and kill me and Rayna.

Grunting in agony, I forced myself up to my knees. I could see the light switch; it was now in reach. I reached up and hit the switch. Subsequently, I heard the boom and the screams. The house was rigged for emergencies just like this. The steel door separated the basement from the rest of the house when the lever was pulled.

Once the lever was pulled, it activated the light switch. Once you hit the light switch, the entire house above was blown up. Shrapnel nails covered every inch of the house, killing everything in the house. You could hear the screams of the guys upstairs as they were being pummeled by thousands of flying nails.

I could hear their screams; followed by the sound of nothingness. I had lost consciousness. The loss of blood and trauma from the fall had won.

"Mr. Stew, get up," were the next words I heard. From total darkness to opening my eyes to see Rayna sitting there, holding me, and telling me to get up. That scene was all too familiar. She held her father the same way. She begged him to get up the same way.

"I told you not to come out," was the first thing I could think to say to her, even though I was glad she did. I am not sure any sight would have been more motivating than waking up to see her holding me.

"We got to get out of here before the police get here," I said to her. She helped me to my feet, as much as any little girl could help a grown man. We walked toward the door as she held my hand; me limping, bleeding, and in pain.

We walked out the backyard to the dock. As we got on the small boat I had, I looked back to see the ruins of what once was my lake house. We could hear the sirens from the fire trucks pulling up as we started the boat.

I drove the boat to the other end of the lake and just pulled up in a wooded area. I could just lay here long enough to gather myself to be able to get out of this neighborhood. We docked the boat, and I laid down just off the edge of the lake. Rayna came over to lay next to me, hugging my neck. I pulled out the emergency cell phone stored in the boat, pinged Stephanie my location before everything faded to black.

I opened my eyes and the first thing I noticed was I was no longer lying by the lake. I could see a ceiling fan above me as the blades were slowly turning. I looked down and saw Rayna was lying in bed next to me.

I went to move my arm and could feel something pull. I looked at my arm and saw I was hooked up to an IV drip. Then Stephanie walked in.

"Looks like you are finally awake."

My vision started clearing and my memory started returning. I looked around the room and realized I was not in a hospital, but in a bedroom. Then Dr. Green walked in the room. Dr. Green was a physician from Barbados. He got caught up in some illegal business here in the states and got his medical license stripped.

Since then, he has been the go-to doctor for the underground world for those who don't want to go to a hospital for legal or safety reasons. Stephanie knew of him and knew taking me to a hospital was not a good idea.

"Mr. Stewart, glad to see you are still here with us," Dr. Green greeted me in a not-so-amusing way. He walked over and opened the curtains. The sun came beaming through the windows as I looked out and saw palm trees and the ocean on the horizon.

"Stephanie, where are we?" I said to her as I tried to sit up. I felt extreme pain in my midsection from trying to sit up. I tried to grab my side, and Dr. Green grabbed my arm.

"Just relax. No sudden movements," he said. There were no palm trees nor oceans in Atlanta, so I knew this was not home.

"We had to get you out of Atlanta," Stephanie spoke up. "Rayna, go in the other room and watch TV for a second, sweetheart," she asked Rayna.

"Can I just go to the beach instead?" she asked. "You can go outside, but you know not to go past the gate," she told her as Rayna opened the door to run outside.

Stephanie told me that there were lots of people looking for me in Atlanta; therefore, she had to get me out of town because they would find me sooner or later.

"Dr. Green loaded you on his boat and took you back to his homeland for safety," she said. I looked at her and then looked out the window.

"His homeland?" I questioned.

"Welcome to beautiful Barbados," Dr. Green said, pointing to the beautiful views from the window.

"Barbados?" I questioned. "If I am in Barbados, how long have I been asleep?"

Dr. Green responded, "You have been in a coma for almost two weeks now. We were worried you were not going to make it for awhile."

I thought to myself, the last thing I recalled was laying down next to Rayna at the lake house in Gwinnett County. I woke up a half a world away on a beach in Barbados. I could feel the pain again on my side as they saw me squirm.

"You are going to need to relax. You are going to have a long and hard recovery," Dr. Green stated. "You had a lot of internal damage." I rested my head back on the pillow and turned to look out the window and saw Rayna outside the window playing. That brought a smile to my face.

"How is she," I asked turning to Stephanie.

"She is a resilient young girl. She would not leave your side. She lay next to you every night, hugging you," she told me. "I don't know what type of bond you have with that little girl, but I can tell you that you are the world to her."

That made me smile as I watched her outside. As much as she had been through and as much of it being the result of my actions, I was happy that I was the one who was able to provide joy for her.

For the next week, this was my life. Lying in bed, looking out the window at the sun, the trees, and the ocean while I watched Rayna play. I did not have the strength to get out of bed. I just lay there sleeping and eating.

A few more days passed, and again I was looking outside at the water and skies. I saw Rayna out there playing in the sand. I wanted to join her, so I rolled myself to the edge of the bed. I grabbed the cane that had been sitting there waiting for me to garner enough strength to use it.

I pulled myself out of the bed and gingerly walked out of the door towards the beach. It was the first time walking in over a month. Step by agonizing step, I walked across the beach to reach her playing in the sand. Rayna looked up and was surprised to see me standing there. She jumped up and ran to hug me. Every time she hugged me, I felt rejuvenated, and the unconditional love she shared made me feel whole.

As I sat in the sand with Rayna, I could see Dr. Green approaching with two men. It was concerning to me, because I had not seen anybody else at the house, and nobody should have known I was there. Who were these two men with Dr. Green? I was about to find out.

"Stew, this is Gerald and Rob," Dr. Green said, pointing to the two of them. I did not acknowledge nor respond as I waited for the rest of the introduction, the part where he told me why they were there.

"I am glad you got out of bed today," he continued. "They are former US Navy Seals. They are here to put you through physical therapy and some training to have you back up and ready to return to the US," he said to me.

I looked at them both as they did not speak. Both were black men who looked to be in excellent physical condition. Both looked as if they carried no body fat and muscles bulged from their shirts.

"They currently do some and physical therapy and private training for US special forces," he told me. "These two are going to have you back doing your job in better shape than you have ever been," he continued. I looked at both, seemingly expressionless faces.

Gerald reached down and pulled up my shirt to see the wounds. "Is this it? I thought you said this man got shot. Getting hit with them little handguns isn't getting shot. Get your lazy ass up and start training," he said, totally catching me off guard.

He was that type of trainer; he was about to try and shame me back into shape. "I got shot with a torpedo and had to carry this fat-ass five miles back to the base," Gerald said, pointing to Rob. Rob just shook his head as if he had heard these stories before.

"Just ignore him, please. He has an active imagination and a warped sense of humor," Rob said to me. "What have you gotten yourself into? Seems like somebody was serious about trying to take you out. The fact that you are now all the way here in Barbados, I guess they got some serious clout to get the job done," he said to me.

I just looked at him. That was a rhetorical question. A man of his experience knew I was not going to answer it. He extended his arm, offering to help me up.

"Let's get back so we can start with your physical therapy." They went on to explain that Gerald was an expert in physical therapy for gunshots and other types of trauma to those in the military. Rob was a hand-to-hand and weapons combat trainer. He traveled the world training elite forces for various governments.

They helped me back to the room, and I sat down on the bed.

"You are completely recovered internally. There is no further risk of damage. How soon you are back on your feet and in top shape is strictly up to you from here," Gerald said. "I can only push you as far as you are willing to go," he continued.

"We already know your story. In our world, we don't get involved with anybody unless we know everything. I can tell you we know everything, and that is why we are both here," Rob said. "We lost a good friend back in Atlanta, and all signs point to this same covert operation" Rob went on to say. "So, getting you healthy enough to return and expose them is a little personal to us also," he said.

I put on my tennis shoes, looked down at the bandages around my midsection, and stood up.

"Good, now let's start this road to recovery," Gerald said.

CHAPTER 10

PREPARING FOR WAR

One thing about life is, time won't stop for anybody. You are either going to use your time well, or time will use you. I looked out the window and saw the sun rise over the horizon, as it glistened over the waters of the Atlantic Ocean creating a picture-perfect view. That view reminded me that it was time for me to start using my time and stop letting time use me.

"Let's , Gerald," I said as I gingerly made my way to the door. I walked out past the kitchen where Rayna was sitting. She stood up when she saw me walking. She was probably more shocked and excited than anyone, as that was her first time seeing me walk on my own since that day.

Gerald and I walked out the door. Rayna ran to her room, grabbed her shoes, and ran out the door behind us. As I walked to the beach, I saw Rob was already there working out. You could tell by the amount of sweat; he had been at it for a while.

"So are you ready to get off your ass," Rob said. "Let's go," as he started a slow jog toward the ocean. I looked around and saw Gerald pointing in that direction as if he was telling me to hurry and follow.

I started to run and felt an unbearable pain shoot through my body. But I pressed on and took another step. I was not going to delay this another day.

I closed my eyes and could see the picture. The blood dripping, her dimple, his hand holding her decapitated head. It reminded me why today I could no longer wait. It reminded me why today I must hit this road to recovery, because they have taken so much from me, and I need to prepare to go and take it back.

Each day it became easier to run. The pain lessened each day and my motivation became stronger. Each day, Gerald and Rob had me in the ocean for hours at a time exercising and building back my strength. And each day we were in the ocean I could see Rayna on the beach watching us, and emulating the things we were doing.

After a few weeks, I felt no effects from the shootings, I felt as if I was back at full strength. I felt like I was ready to head back to the States and wage war on everything and everybody involved.

"Rob, I think I am going to go back to the States this weekend," I stated. He did not respond; he simply took another drink from his cup. Gerald walked into the room, and Rob turned to him, "He thinks he is ready to go now," he said to Gerald.

"Good, we can finish the workout today since he is ready," Gerald stated.

We headed down to the beach as usual. We were in the water, high energy non-stop movement like every other day. My mind started to drift, thinking about returning home for revenge. I felt I was ready and in as good of shape as I have ever been.

"You think you are ready?" Gerald said to me as we paused.

"Yeah, never been more prepared in my life," I responded.

As soon as I finished that sentence, my legs were pulled from under me falling face first in the water. I felt an arm wrapped around my throat as I was underwater trying to regain my bearings. I reached up to try and pull the arm away from my throat, and they tightened their grip.

I was being held underwater and choked. I tried to loosen the grip around my neck and push to get my head above water at the same time. It was fruitless, as I had no leverage to rise out of the water and no strength to overcome the chokehold.

I was choking and drowning at the same time. And then I lost consciousness.

"Wake up," I heard as I felt a thump to my back. The punch to my back knocked the fluids out of me and back to consciousness. There was ocean water flowing from my mouth and nose while I was gagging and choking. After a few more seconds of trying to catch my breath, I focused my eyes and saw Rob standing in front of me.

"And you think you are ready," Gerald said in a sarcastic tone.

"You would be dead right now, but you are ready, huh," Rob stated.

"I thought you had been trained for this. You are simply a street fighter with no awareness," Gerald said.

Rob snuck up on me as their way of showing me that I was not ready. I do not think they could have proved their point any better than damn near killing me in the middle of the ocean.

"You have been trained to fight. You can teach a monkey how to fight. The key is being taught how to survive," Rob emphasized.

"You can go back to America half prepared, and eventually somebody else will be taking care of Baby Girl, or you can stay here for a while and really prepare for surviving war," Gerald said.

I felt that I was one of the baddest men on earth and could stand toe to toe with any man. Somehow, these two made me feel inferior, as there was a lot left for me to learn. The fact that I let Rob disappear in the water and never noticed, struck a chord that I needed more training.

I was ready to take the next step with Gerald and Rob.

Day after day of training, learning, and preparing, there was one thing that stayed consistent with them. Never stop observing your surroundings, and never stop thinking about a plan, cover, and counter to an attack at any moment. They spent most of their time teaching mental awareness and self-defense.

It was very tiring training with them trying to recover from the injuries. But training with them to go to war, was even worse. It was exhausting, and each day I made it back to the house ready to pass out.

After a session, I sat down on the couch and fell asleep there. Rayna walked in and saw me sleeping on the couch. She went and grabbed a blanket, curled up next to me, and pulled the blanket over both of us. Her laying on me woke me, and I just looked at her.

I put my arm around her and kissed her on the forehead. I had developed such a strong love for this little girl. I loved her more than any man could love his daughter. I could feel from her touch and the look in her eyes, that I meant the world to her.

"Mr. Stew," Rayna said as I looked down at her lying against my chest.

"Why have so many people I loved died? Have I done something wrong? Can you promise that you won't leave me too?" Rayna blurted out.

I felt bad for her. At such a young age, she had lost both parents and Kim. She had seen more death than most people twice her age. I did not know how to answer her question, I could not make a promise I couldn't keep.

It was an awkward moment of silence.

"I will do everything I can to have you never experience that kind of hurt again. I promise to protect you."

She sat up and looked at me. "I promise next time somebody comes after you, I will help you and not make you fight alone."

I looked at her. She meant every word she said, she meant in her heart she was ready to fight to protect me, the last adult in her life.

"I don't need you to help me fight anybody. I need you to stay safe, go to school and get your education and live out your dreams."

That moment with Rayna gave me life. She became the reason I had to live. She became the reason I had to smile. She became my everything and I wanted to protect her from any more hurt.

We fell asleep on the couch. Rayna clung to me like a security blanket as she slept. I was happy to give her that type of comfort and enjoyed every moment of watching her sleep. I have no idea what it was like to have your own kids, but I cannot imagine any parent feeling any more love for a child than I have for Rayna.

The rising sun peeking through the window woke me. I sat up and the movement woke Rayna. I stood and grabbed my shoes.

"I am about to go run the beach," I said to Rayna, wanting to get to the beach to run against the backdrop of the sun rising.

"Wait, I am coming," Rayna said as she scrambled to find her shoes.

I ran out to the beach with Rayna following behind me. I would run from the house to the lighthouse and back past the house to the dock, then back home. That was the routine every morning. That was two and a half miles on the beach, in the sand.

I took off running and so did Rayna. She would keep up with me if she could before she would be all behind. That was a long run for a girl her age, but she finished it every morning with me. I would then spend time shadowboxing, kickboxing, and just generally training alone on the beach as she sat and watched.

That was my morning routine before Gerald and Rob arrived later for their sessions each day. I felt like they had trained me to be some cross between a hardened street fighter and an experienced Navy Seal. I left another exhausting training session and Rayna, and I walked up the beach back to the house.

When we arrived, Stephanie was sitting at the table alone. From the look on her face, we could tell something was wrong. Rayna ran up to her, "What is wrong Ms. Stephanie."

Stephanie told Rayna to go to the room so we could speak. Rayna looked around and walked toward the door to the other room. As Rayna walked through the doorway, she just leaned up against the wall to try and hear what was being said.

"Look at this," Stephanie said as she handed me the phone. It was a news clip of a house explosion back in Atlanta. I zoomed in on the video, "is this your house," I said in shock.

This was no coincidence; Command must know that Stephanie helped me.

"Was anybody there?" I asked her.

"My friend Breunna was in town and there. She was staying at the house this week to watch it while we were gone, you know the crazy thing is, we look a lot alike," Stephanie said on the verge of tears.

They must have thought it was Stephanie and tried to kill her. That meant they were going after everybody associated with me and the explosion was meant to send a message. They know I survived, and they are not going to stop until they locate me. They are not going to stop until they kill me, or I kill them. ALL of them.

"Some days I wonder if my life would not be easier if I was still sitting in that jail cell and never took this job," I said to Stephanie questioning everything that has happened. "You know how many families have held funerals because of me and Ghost Squad? It was not just the criminals, they had me going after good, hard-working people. You know how many other kids like Rayna that must be out there who lost their parents for no reason at all, but for crossing the wrong people."

Rayna just stood on the wall listening. Reliving the day, she sat there and saw her dad get killed. Questioning the truth behind why he was killed, because all she knows is that nobody was ever arrested for his murder.

Rayna began to cry as she was leaning on the wall eavesdropping. I could hear her at the door, and I looked at Stephanie. I wondered what she heard. Does she know anything about who killed her dad? I reluctantly walked towards the doorway, not knowing what I would say to her. Nervous that she may know the truth.

"Rayna," I said as I reached the door.

She burst into tears and ran to hug me. She held me tight as she cried. I was at a loss for words, so I just hugged her back. We stood there without saying a word as Stephanie looked on.

I picked Rayna up and carried her to the couch. We sat down and I tried to think of a way to have a conversation with her about everything that was going on.

"Mr. Stew, why is there so much violence around me? Sometimes I feel like I am cursed. The thought of violence does not even bother me anymore. It is the thought that I am cursed, and death follows me is what bothers me," explained Rayna.

I was in complete shock. To hear those words come from the mouth of an innocent, precious little girl was heartbreaking.

"I knew my Daddy was going to die. I heard him telling somebody he had done too many bad things in life, and he knew somebody would come and get him for them one day." Rayna said. "He was still my daddy, and I did not want him to die. I just wanted him to stop doing bad things. And when I saw that man leaving the room, I knew who it was."

My heart stopped. "What do you mean you knew who it was," I asked nervously.

How would I explain to her why I did it? She knew all this time and never said anything to me. She treated me like her father, and knew the whole time I was the one that killed her dad? My mind was racing, and my palms started to sweat.

Nothing had made me as nervous as I was at that moment. I always knew there may come a time that we would have to talk about this, but I knew I was never going to be prepared to discuss it, and definitely not like this.

"Listen, Rayna," I nervously began, not knowing what I would say next.

"I did not know *WHO* it was, but I knew it was somebody coming to get my daddy," Rayna uttered giving me a sense of relief. She knew it was somebody coming to kill her dad, but she did not know it was me. That was a relief, but I still knew we would have to discuss this one day, but today is not that day.

Back in Atlanta, Command was on a warpath searching for me and anybody associated with me. I heard of them torturing and questioning any and everybody that could possibly know me. They knew I survived, and they were not going to stop until they found me.

I had not reached out to anybody in the States to let them know any details, so there was nothing for anybody to tell. I made sure that Stephanie did the same, as far as everybody knows we just disappeared.

Command was getting messy and loud as they tried to cover their tracks. Rumors started circulating heavily of a rogue police unit that was terrorizing and killing people. The more the word got out, the more people Command tried to silence. It was as if they had engaged in a war against the entire city.

I had to put an end to this, I had to get back to the States. It had been six months and Command had come unhinged. The bombing of Stephanie's house was a sign of desperation and let me know they were as reckless as they were focused.

Over a decade ago the Ghost Squad was started with good intentions. A young gang-banging thug started his own gang called the IGs, or International Gangsters. They were young and very violent. It started out as just some corner boys selling weed and it escalated to a group that had the entire city in fear.

They got a taste for blood, and it was never enough. Rumor has it that Foot, the leader of this crew was at the store, and somebody stepped on his tennis shoes. Foot and his crew jumped on the kid, and he hit his head on a curb killing him. This was the start of the rampage that went on throughout the city.

There was a witness that spoke to the police about the fight. The IGs tracked down the witness and cut his head off. They walked through the projects with the head and stuck it on a pole in the middle of the projects with a sign around the pole that read "Snitches."

Going after people like Foot and the IGs was the original purpose of the Ghost Squad. To use unconventional tactics to curb violent crime.

How did it possibly go so far off course? The thoughts of the drastic change in the intent for Ghost Squad and what it has become, had me thinking about the changes I had made in life. Looking at Rayna and then I started to think back on my days in jail.

Thoughts go back to those cold gray bars. Being forced to sit in this small concrete room the size of some people's closet. Decorated with this ugly iron bunk bed, that took up half the room and was bolted to the floor with rusted iron screws.

There was a stainless-steel toilet only inches away from the bed. The toilet looked as if it had barely survived a decade's worth of fecal matter and urine deposits. Any human being would likely get sick with just the thought of sitting on such a germ-infested piece of metal, but as a prisoner that was all you had.

More stainless-steel décor was the desk and stool combination that was bolted to the wall, taking up whatever area of that part of the cell the bunk beds left available.

You had nothing to do as you were locked in the cell but to sleep or do whatever limited exercises you could achieve in such a confined space. Just lay in bed looking at the graffiti-filled walls and ceilings. Lined with messages, gang tags, and anything else a person could write on a wall or carve into the desk or bed.

Then there were the screams. There were the screams of the crazies that you could hear at any time day or night. Not screaming at anything or anybody, or maybe there were voices in their heads they were screaming at. You could look out your cell and see some of the crazies at their cell door constantly fighting the air, yelling at the air. And the guards just looked on as if this was normal.

There were the other screams you would hear. Ones from guys that may have crossed the wrong person or just been in the wrong place and were dealt with the only way prisoners know how, violence. I saw too many people get beaten, even to death, and nobody would step in to stop it.

In prison, it was the law. If it didn't involve you, you didn't interject yourself into it. Mind your business and whatever else is happening, you didn't see it.

Then there were the other screams. You get hundreds of testosterone-filled alpha males all locked in confined spaces together without being able to touch or feel a woman, they compromise. Any person walking the halls of the prison who does not display the bravado and tendencies of an alpha male soon becomes a target.

If you are in prison and show any form of weakness, somebody will pick up on it. If you show any signs that something bothers you in this place, they will exploit that as a weakness. They will test you. And if you don't respond the right way, they will push it even further. The next thing you know, there is no respect for you as a man, and they treat you as such.

It is a shame to see grown men forced into sexual submission as a form of survival. And those screams you hear are of those that make their futile attempts to resist it. That experience has broken many men. Some give up and concede. Some would rather end it all than be forced to do such things. And then you got some that lose it totally. They turn into psych patients or worse, revenge-seeking savages.

I stayed to myself in prison, but every man that walks through those doors at one point or another has to prove himself. It is simply a rite of passage. You got to show that you can, will, and know how to successfully defend yourself, even to the point of killing.

"Stewart, you are too good to come out and eat with us," he said as he walked by my cell. Two hours of free time, and I spent most of it each day in my cell eating those god-awful sandwiches they served us for lunch most days.

I just looked up at him, I knew that this was a precursor to a showdown he had in store for me. They called him Tay. He was one of the young wild kids that always felt that he had to prove his superiority and dominance in the pod.

"So, you just going to look and not respond," he went further.

"I guess we need to see if that mouth even works," Tay said. That was a gauntlet he was throwing down. That statement let me know, the next time I see him, I have to make my point before he did. And chances are, he probably was not coming alone.

The next day I heard the buzz. Then the sound of metal clinging as the locks on the cell doors were released. I knew that when the doors opened, he was coming back and not talking this time. I went and put a shirt in the stainless-steel sink clogging the drain as I turned on the water.

I took a couple of magazines and wrapped them around my stomach and tied them tightly with my extra t-shirt. As the water in the sink began to fill, I started splashing water all over the concrete floor. Those concrete floors were coated for durability, but once they were wet, they became extremely slippery.

Just as I expected, Tay came walking toward my cell.

"Stewart, you still in your cell," I could hear Tay as his voice got closer to my cell.

Then, there he was with one other guy standing at the door of my cell. I was standing between my bed and the desk, ready to take on whatever was before me. Tay came running into my cell at me. I grabbed the desk with one hand and the bed with the other for leverage and kicked him right in the chest as he ran toward me.

The kick knocked him backward hitting the ground as you could see the water from the floor splash up while he was sliding across the floor on his back. I went charging after the second guy as he was reaching down to try and pick Tay up.

I landed a knee to his head knocking him back into the walkway and against the iron rail. This bully was about to get everything he wanted and more today.

As everybody in the common area scrambled to get a better view, I jumped on top of Tay and began to punch him relentlessly one after another. His partner had gathered himself and landed a powerful right to my jaw, knocking me backwards into the cell.

As I was laying on the floor in the cell, he tried to jump over a semi-conscious Tay coming towards me, but when he landed on the wet floor he slipped and fell backward. I jumped on top of him and landed a hard right. Then I put my hands around his neck and began to choke him.

I didn't realize he was reaching for a shank he had in his waistband while I was on top of him. He took the shank and jammed it into my side. His shank had to penetrate about three layers of magazines, so it merely broke my skin. I then slammed his head against the concrete floor knocking him unconscious.

I walked over to Tay as he was trying to gather himself, and I punched him knocking him backward and unconscious in the walkway. I went and grabbed the other guy by the back of his shirt and dragged him out of my cell, throwing him on top of Tay.

I looked up to see dozens of eyes watching this all unfold. I went in and grabbed the shank while everybody looked on. I took the shank and threw it across the pod.

About that time I heard the sirens ring out throughout the pod. When everybody heard that siren, they knew to lie down. Everybody in the pod was lying face down on the floor in the common area and the tactical force of guards came rushing through the door to the pod.

I turned and walked back to my bed and lay there. I felt at peace, as I knew that would be the last time in jail anybody would try me for just being me.

And now I had come full circle. This time it was not a bully in a cell, but an entire unit I was going to have to man up and take on to rid myself of this problem once and for all.

Just as I had strapped up and prepared that day in the cell, I got to strap up and prepare for a war against Ghost Squad one last time.

CHAPTER 11

WELCOME HOME

After months of recovery and intense training, Gerald and Rob agreed the time had come. I had reached a place mentally and physically where I was prepared to return to Atlanta. It was time to return and face Command to rid this city of the most treacherous gang it has faced. One last night here in paradise before we head back.

Gerald and Rob planned a barbeque at the house for our last day. Just a time for us to enjoy the beach and the scenery together. As I walked out of the house, I could smell the aroma of something on the grill. I am not sure what was on the grill, but it smelled delicious.

Rayna ran up behind me and grabbed me. "Mr. Stew, what are they cooking? It smells good."

"Hey baby girl. I don't know but yes it does," I said to her.

I turned to give her a hug and then I noticed. I guess through it all, I had not noticed she was growing up very fast before my eyes. I took a step back to look at her.

"Wow! Baby girl." I said to Rayna.

"What is wrong?" she questioned as she looked down at herself, trying to see what I could be looking at.

I just looked at her. From her feet where she wore beach shoes that were a little too small. Her feet were bigger than the shoes. I looked up and saw the development in her legs. All the days running behind me, she was getting her personal workout, and you could see the change in her body.

Looking at the shoes I told her, "I am going to buy you some new shoes when we get home," I was amazed at how much she had grown.

I reached up and put my hands on her shoulders and could feel the muscular development. I took a step back to get a better look.

"Wow…just wow." I said again. Rayna looked perplexed as to what I could be thinking.

"Is something wrong?" Rayna asked me.

"Nothing is wrong at all. Just I have been so focused on my recovery, I have not realized you have grown about three inches within the last few months and have gotten yourself in very good shape." I said, astonished I have just noticing the growth.

She had gone from a skinny pre-teen to an athletic teenager overnight.

"You just look so beautiful…and grown all of a sudden," I told Rayna.

"Mr. Stew, yes I have gone through some changes the last few months," Rayna said as Stephanie walked up.

"Yeah Stew, she has gone through a lot of changes. She has become a woman." Stephanie added.

"Yes, I got my first-" Rayna started before I cut her off.

"Whoa, that is enough. I think I heard enough, and I get the point." I said as I had no desire to hear what she was about to say. "Let's just go eat, geez," I said sarcastically, trying to end that subject.

Grabbing Rayna, we started walking towards the beach and the food. While we were walking, Stephanie grabbed my other hand.

I looked down and saw us holding hands, as it caught me off guard. I looked up and our eyes caught one another. It was an awkward moment. I quickly looked away like a confused shy little boy, scared to look into her eyes.

I did not know whether to pull my hand away, or just keep walking. But we had made it to the beach, and I quickly pulled my hand away to hug and thank Gerald and Rob for everything.

"You guys do not know how much I appreciate everything you have done for me," I paused as I looked back at Rayna and Stephanie. "Done for us." I corrected myself.

"Let's just eat," I blurted out. "And what do you all have on the grill? Whatever it is smells so damn good." I exclaimed, anxious to see what was on the grill.

Rob opened the top of the grill, and you could see a whole roasted pig inside. I never had a pig roast before, but if it tasted half as good as it smelled I was going to be in for a treat.

We all took a seat at the table on the beach. Stephanie sat next to me, and I looked at her. Our eyes connected, and again I quickly looked away. It was uncomfortable looking into her eyes the way we held hands walking to the beach.

"Everybody dig in!" I uttered, trying to break the uneasy feeling I was experiencing.

The pig was every bit as good as it smelled. It was the most juicy and flavorful meat I had ever eaten.

"Rob, this is delicious!" I expressed, as the flavor of the meat exploded in my mouth. I was not sure how I had ever neglected to treat myself to such a delicious delicacy before.

We ate and enjoyed the view, knowing this would be our last night. It could not have been a more perfect night view for a sendoff party.

I stood up to make a toast. I toasted to friends, and to Rob and Gerald for their hospitality and dedication to getting me healthy.

"Cheers!" everybody said as I finished my speech.

Rob spoke up. "Gerald and I have been talking. We think we should go back to the states with you."

"No, I do not want you all to get wrapped up in all of this. It is my mess to straighten out." I explained to them.

"You didn't ask us to come, we are asking you. Besides, we would just be here bored out of our minds with nothing to do." Rob explained.

"Still, I do not want to drag anybody else into this mess I got myself into," I emphasized to them.

I was going to stand firm that I did not want them involved; though I knew their help would change the odds dramatically. They saw I was firm and would not bend on this topic.

"Ok, we get it. Just know we are one phone call away if you change your mind." Gerald said.

"Before you go though, we have something for you to remember us," Rob stated. Gerald grabbed a box from a nearby bag.

"You didn't have to give me any gifts," I replied.

"Don't consider it a gift. More so a good luck charm." Gerald said as he handed the box to me.

I was shocked they had given me a gift, and was curious to know what it could be. I looked at the box, before I started tearing it open. I opened the box and pulled it out. It was two gray hoodies. I just smiled at the thought of it.

"We figured you could use a new hoodie for work." Rob joked. Indeed, I needed a new hoodie, and these two were just what I needed.

"Thank you both!" I exclaimed as the moment and the meaning of putting back on the gray hoodie hit me.

We wrapped up, then cleaned our mess before heading back to the house.

"Step, can I speak to you a moment before we go back in?" I nervously expressed. I knew I needed to have a conversation with her which could not wait any longer.

As everybody else walked back to the house, we walked further out towards the water. I sat down just beyond the edge of the water line. Stephanie sat down next to me.

"Stew, I agree. We need to talk." Stephanie said as she sat down.

"OK, you go first. What did you need to talk about?" I gave her the opportunity.

"No, you asked to talk, so I will let you begin." she replied.

Reluctantly, I agreed, and I started. "When we return to Atlanta, there are going to be eyes all over the place looking for us, and I need to tell you what I need you and Rayna to do."

I had a plan all laid out to keep her and Rayna out of harm's way until this entire episode was over. I explained to her where she needed to go. I gave her a note with a phone number for me that only she would have. I gave instructions on what to do when we get there. Who to talk to. Who to not talk to.

I put a lot in her lap as I continuously talked, trying to get her to understand what we were about to face, and the importance of her following my instructions. She listened intently and I felt she understood the urgency of it all.

We sat going over the plan again and again until I was sure she understood what to do, and what the emergency plan would be in case anything went wrong. We sat there for forty-five minutes going over everything.

"I think you got it." I expressed to her when I felt comfortable.

"Let's head back in to finish packing." I stated as we got up and headed back to the house. "Oh, what is it you wanted to talk about?"

She paused and looked at me. "You know what. It is not important. It can wait," she said as we walked into the house.

The next morning, we loaded up everything and headed to the airport. We were taking a flight to Orlando, and then driving back to Atlanta. We could not take the chance of trying to fly into Atlanta; having them spot us in the airport.

We had fake passports and names to get into the country undetected. We arrived in Orlando without any problems. I was on high alert, cautiously surveying our surroundings. It was interesting watching Rayna. She seemed to be very alert to her surroundings.

We left the rental car center and were off on the six-hour drive back to Atlanta. The drive would give me time to think. Time to recall all the harm Ghost Squad had done to the people in the city, and reflect on what is important to me now.

While there in Barbados, I realized Stephanie and Rayna were all I had left in life. I looked at them in the car as they slept, and understood this was my family. I needed to put an end to this drama, so they could live in peace.

As we approached the Atlanta area, I could sense myself becoming more focused; starting to really lock in on the task at hand. I had gotten a rental property in the suburbs of Atlanta where Stephanie and Rayna would stay to be out of harm's way.

Meanwhile, as expected, Command had tapped into all resources to locate me. Ghost Squad had gotten a hit on the FAA facial recognition software in Orlando airport.

As Command sat behind the desk, a picture was dropped. Ghost Squad had now identified me, and a picture of Stephanie and Rayna also. As I hid them out in the suburbs, little did I know they had already been identified by Ghost Squad, and were equally being sought.

We finally arrived at the house. I took a moment to relax as Stephanie and Rayna unpacked and settled in. It was late in the evening, and the thought was to rest for the night to start fresh in the morning.

Rayna was sitting in the backyard under the moonlit sky. I looked at the beautiful young teen she had grown into in such a short period of time. I walked out and took a seat next to her.

"You know, I have to leave in the morning. As we previously discussed, you all will have to keep out of sight for a while until everything settles down." I said to Rayna as we sat looking into the night sky.

"Mr. Stew," Rayna started. "You know I know a lot more about what is going on than everybody thinks. Everybody treats me like a little kid, and I am not a little kid anymore." she calmly, but emphatically said.

"The things I have seen in life, and the thoughts I have in my head; they are not the same things other teenage girls think about." Rayna exclaimed.

"I want revenge. I want to take down everything that has taken something from me. I mean the system, not the people. Whoever killed my dad, they were just part of the system. I want to take down the system that allows this stuff to continue to happen in our world." Rayna said as her voice began to fill with emotion.

I reached over and put my arm around her.

"Baby girl, leave all of that to me. All that rage and revenge you may have, let me carry it for you. I will get the revenge you seek. I will handle the system you want to take down. I just want you to try and be as normal of a teenage kid as you can be." I uttered trying to calm her.

I had never seen that look on her face before. Returning to Atlanta changed my focus and mindset for what I needed to accomplish, but I had never thought about how returning here would affect her.

"You just don't get it. I am going to bed." Rayna said as she got up and headed back into the house. I sat there for a minute thinking about what had just transpired. I could only imagine her thoughts, and I was still nervous about what she may know. We are going to have to discuss that sooner than later.

I walked back into the house to find Stephanie sitting on the couch.

"What was that about?" she stated, obviously referring to Rayna storming into the house and to her room.

"She is just a teenager dealing with a lot of emotions right now." I told Stephanie, downplaying what was going through Rayna's head.

I sat down on the couch next to Stephanie.

"Are you OK? How are you dealing with everything?" I asked her to make sure I did not take her mindset for granted.

"I am scared." Stephanie said.

"We all have lost so much, sacrificed so much, and now it seems like we are all we have left. And you are going to walk out this door in the morning with no guarantee you will ever return." Stephanie emotionally vented as a tear formed in her eye.

"Don't think like that." I responded as I reached over to grab her hand to comfort her.

Stephanie looked up at me and I saw that look in her eyes again. Then she leaned in and kissed me. I froze, not knowing how to respond. We had known each other since we were little kids and had never shared those types of emotions.

She reached up, put her hand behind my head, and held me closer as she continued to kiss me. I was pleasantly shocked, yet confused. As she continued kissing me, I felt my state of confusion turning into one of reciprocal passion. I pulled her closer and then began returning the passion, the energy.

I stood up as we were still passionately intertwined and started backing towards the bedroom. The intensity in the kisses increased with every step we took. I began unbuttoning her shirt as I backed towards the door. She reached down and began unzipping my pants.

We reached the bedroom, I pushed the door shut, and pinned her against the door. I grabbed both of her arms pinning them above her head against the door, exposing her breast as her shirt was fully unbuttoned.

I slowly kissed her on the chin, then her neck, and gently ran my tongue lower until I reached her nipples to passionately suck on her breast. I could feel her breathing getting heavier.

I reached down and untied the drawstring to her shorts, and they fell to the ground. Slowly I pulled down her underwear while passionately kissing her breast. Her underwear hit the ground and I picked her up as she wrapped her legs around me.

As she was pinned against the door, I felt myself sliding inside of her. I saw her eyes roll in her head and heard her moan. She began to thrust her hips against me as I held her in the air against the door.

I carried her from the door to the bed with her legs still wrapped around me. We were now on the bed as I passionately thrust myself deeper and deeper inside of her. The more I moved, the more passionately she responded.

I was about to explode; I was being mentally and physically fulfilled simultaneously. She was breathing faster and heavier. She let out a scream, as she tried to catch herself, remembering we were not alone in the house. Then she lost it. I felt her release all her passion and juices on me, just as I was doing the same. We arrived at the same time.

I was sweating and looked at her. We had never crossed this line before. I gave her a kiss and rolled over. She laid her head on my chest, put her leg over me, and we fell asleep holding one another.

"Gross!" was the next thing I heard. I woke up to see Rayna standing in the doorway. Stephanie and I just looked at each other and laughed after She shut the door again. I scrambled to my feet to check the time. It was 5:30 in the morning.

We got dressed and walked out to see Rayna sitting in the kitchen.

"Y'all are gross." She said without even looking up.

I tried to hide the fact I was laughing inside at her reaction, while trying to stay stoic. You could see the embarrassment on Stephanie's face. We all sat down and at that moment I realized not only were we all each other had; we were our own dysfunctional family.

They were to go to the grocery store that morning, then remain at the house and out of public sight. They drove the rental car. We had arranged a motorcycle for me.

I grabbed the box Gerald and Rob had given me; putting it into my backpack. I hopped on the motorcycle and headed to the storage room I had always kept. I got to the storage room and looked around to make sure nobody was looking as I opened the door.

When I let the door up, I could see everything was in order as I had left it. I pulled the door back down behind me and turned on the light. There you could see a storage room which served as my personal armory.

Back in the suburbs, Stephanie and Rayna headed off to the store. Stephanie was still uncomfortable about that morning.

"Rayna, about this morning," Stephanie started before Rayna cut her off.

"No need to explain. It was gross, but it was long overdue." Rayna said, speaking like a person well beyond her years.

This embarrassed Stephanie even more. She was speechless and didn't know how to respond.

"Everybody knew you two were falling in love, except for y'all," Rayna stated as if she was frustrated that she had to explain.

"Well, what do you want to get from the store?" Stephanie said, trying to change the topic.

They arrived at the store as Stephanie was still embarrassed about the things this teenager had seen and spoke. Rayna was quiet most of the ride, constantly looking in the mirror, checking things out along the route.

As they parked to go into the store, a gray Honda passed them, parking a few spaces away. They walked into the store and Rayna noticed nobody had gotten out of the car; but, she did get a glance at the person driving and could tell two others were in the car.

She remained quiet and alert as they shopped, while she pushed the cart. Stephanie was oblivious to everything, but Rayna was super-observant and alert. As they were walking down the aisle, Rayna saw a guy in a black hoodie walking down the next aisle pushing a cart.

As they turned down another aisle Rayna saw him, and his empty cart went down the aisle, staying one aisle away from them. Stephanie was unaware of anything going on as she continued to shop. Stephanie and Rayna turned another aisle and she saw the man in the black hoodie at the end of the aisle with his empty cart.

This time when they turned the aisle, Rayna grabbed Stephanie's hand and said, "Come on." They ran through the produce doors as Stephanie asked Rayna what was going on.

Rayna led her as they hid behind the walk-in freezer.

"The man in the black hoodie is following us. I saw him in the car with two other people, and now the store," Rayna whispered to her.

"Stay here," Rayna said as she sprinted out of the door back into the store.

"Rayna!" Stephanie yelled, nervous and confused.

Rayna burst through the door and sprinted toward the front door of the store, knocking over a box of cans to cause a commotion. The man in the black hoodie saw this and started running behind her. Rayna sprinted out the door and through the parking lot.

The man in the black hoodie ran out of the store behind her as the Honda peels out of the parking lot.

Rayna ran across the street and into a gas station. She ran through the gas station and out the back door as the guy continues to pursue her.

She ran another block and turned down an alley between two buildings. She checked doors in the alley, and each was locked. There was a ten-foot barbed wire fence at the end of the alley, and all the doors were locked. She had made a wrong turn.

She looked back and saw the guy in the black hoodie turning down the alley, soon followed by the Honda as the other two guys jumped out of it.

She walked backwards until she was against the fence. There was nowhere left for her to go as the three guys were closing in. Rayna got down on both knees with her hands on her head and smiled. She knew the guys were not going to harm her, as they wanted Stew. She was able to lead them away from Stephanie, so she felt accomplished.

The guys grabbed Rayna and threw her into the back of the car, threw a hood over her head before speeding off.

At the store Stephanie ran to the car to grab the phone. She knew we were not to use any phones except for emergencies. Frantically she tried to get to the phone to call me.

"Stew…somebody was following us, and Rayna ran off." Stephanie screamed into the phone. "I don't know where she went."

My heart dropped. That was not what I expected to hear. I figured they would be safe at least for a little while. Not only did Command know I was alive, but they also knew where we were. This meant a change of plan, as we no longer had the element of surprise. Most importantly, I needed to find Rayna. She was smart and had natural survival skills, but I needed to get to her before they did.

I was becoming furious at the thought of them harming her. I had experienced death, loss of loved ones, but the thought of them hurting a kid; this was unimaginable.

Then my phone rang. Only two people had this number, Stephanie and Rayna. Hesitantly, I answered the phone.

"Rayna?" I said in a questioning tone.

But the voice on the other end was not Rayna. It was a male voice.

"You know the drill. Very simple, your life for hers." the voice on the other end stated.

My worst thoughts had been realized. They did have her. She did not get away. I dropped to my knees. This could be the last straw. I already felt I had nothing in life left except Rayna and Stephanie, and they had just taken Rayna.

"Listen carefully," I started. "There won't be an exchange. If you touch her, I will hunt you down and kill everybody in your family to make you feel the pain of knowing you caused the death of your parents, wife, and siblings."

"I do not want you to fear what I may do to you. I want you to know if you don't let her go safe and sound, there is nothing you can do to stop the things I will do to you." I emphasized.

"Welcome home." the voice said and hung up the phone.

Here I stood in the storage room, preparing for war. I gathered an array of weapons. I had gone into a totally different mental space and was laser focused on the mission at hand. There was no way I was going to let Rayna spend a second longer in these guys' hands. After I gathered everything I needed and put it into the duffle bag, I opened the box Rob and Gerald had given me.

I put a black ski mask on. I pulled out the gray hoodie they had given me and put it on. I turned and caught a glance of myself in the mirror. I saw that look in my eyes.

I pulled the hoodie over my head.

"You are right, welcome home. Gray Ghost is back." I said into the mirror.

CHAPTER 12

GHOST HUNTING

I walked out of the storage room and now the game plan has changed. They had Rayna, and now it was time for me to go on the offensive. Ghost Squad was only partially funded by the city. Most of the cash and weapons of Ghost Squad were from seizures and arrests. The bigger the arrest, the more money, and weapons for Ghost Squad. If I wanted to send a message, going after their money and weapons would be the ultimate message.

Ghost Squad had two secret locations where they would stash the proceeds from their heist. Classic City Fine Arts was a fine arts museum to the world. Dignitaries and high society people frequented there and hosted events regularly upstairs, with no idea what secrets were held behind the locked doors. The security and staff at the facility were not your run-of-the-mill art museum staff. They were all trainees with the Ghost Squad, and they had no idea what they were protecting.

The museum was my first stop. In the underground vault, they kept an arsenal of weapons. There were only two ways into the vault, through the museum and the heavily secured entrance or the secret loading area that was used to get weapons in and out of the facility.

The loading dock looked like it was an entrance to the restaurant next door, but a trap door gave you access to the storage vault under the museum.

Getting access to the vault through the loading dock would be much easier than trying to get through the museum with the security there and the vault door. But there are no scheduled times to go in and out. Opening the trap door required a retina scan and door release from a second person at a remote location.

I was pressed for time to save Rayna, but getting in the vault was critical. It also served as the server and communication hub for Ghost Squad. Killing the communication would isolate everybody since all communications within Ghost Squad were done on secure lines.

I parked around the corner from the dock and walked to the dock area trying to avoid being seen by the multiple security cameras. I was going to have to hide out in the dumpster near the loading dock until somebody came to access the vault.

It was a gamble because I would not know when anybody would come and would not know if a person coming was going to the restaurant or to the vault. One of the things you learned on the job was patience. Sometimes you had to sit in a place for days at a time waiting for your target.

Once I broke into the house of a murderous drug lord to wait for him to return. After a day of waiting inside his house, his elderly grandmother and kid returned home without him. As I sat hiding in the guest bedroom, Grandma decided to make that her room for the night. She could not sleep in the bed because of her back, so she slept in a reclining chair.

The chair was pushed up against the closet door with me stuck inside the closet while Grandma slept. After three days in the closet, he finally came home. As they gathered all of Grandma's things for her to leave, I could see him through the crack in the door.

Along with a teenage child, they helped grandma out of the room and to the car for the ride home. They left the suitcase and had to go back into the room to get it. I exited the closet and waited behind the door for them to return the suitcase and hoped it was him and not the teenager. As I hid behind the door, I could hear him approaching on the phone.

He walked into the room, and reached down to pick up the suitcase. I walked behind him, grabbed his forehead and pulled his head back as I sliced his throat. He fell to the floor dropping the phone. I could hear the person on the other end, "Hello? Hello?"

I walked out the back door of the house and down the side of the driveway as the grandma and the teenager sat in the car waiting for him to return with the suitcase. That was 3 days waiting in the closet for one job. You had to learn patience.

After sitting in the dumpster overnight, a truck pulled up as the sun came up. I would have one chance, I had to make sure it was not a delivery truck for the restaurant. If I blew my cover and it was for the restaurant, I would not have another chance to get into the vault from here.

As the man got out of his truck, I did not recognize him. There was also a small kid in the front seat of the truck. He walked to the back of his truck and loaded some carts on a dolly. Watching him through the opening in the dumpster, he looked like an ordinary delivery guy, and he was traveling with a kid. This wasn't my guy.

As he walked past the dumpster pushing his dolly, I noticed his wrist. The delivery guy was wearing a presidential gold Rolex. No delivery driver could afford such a watch, this must be a member of Ghost Squad.

After he walked by, I pushed open the lid of the dumpster and hurried to catch up with him before he could get inside. I had to get close enough to him without being seen. In addition to the retina scan, the voice recognition detected variances in your voice. Any detection of stress or fear in the voice, the door would not be unlocked.

I stood there just out of sight and listening to him.

"Ghost 8, security clearance Kappa, one, nine, one, one. Codeword Indiana," he said as he pressed his eyes into the retina scanner.

"Identity authenticated. Access granted," the computer-generated voice stated. As soon as I heard the locking mechanism click, I rushed from behind the wall, grabbing him from behind, and pushing him into the room.

"What the hell?" he said as he felt the barrel of my gun against his head and my arm around his neck.

I knocked him to the floor, and he rolled over to see me.

"Gray Ghost," he said with astonishment. "I have heard so much about you, and we have to meet like this."

"Sit up," I said as I pulled out some zip ties. "Well, I hate we had to meet like this, but I am going to take down Command and everything associated with it, so I guess that includes you too," I stated as I taped his mouth shut.

He sat there, bound and gagged, watching me load up some weapons in a duffle bag. He watched as I placed explosives on the server and the communications tower. I could hear him mumbling but tried to pay him no attention. I needed to hurry before they got too anxious and did something to Rayna.

I gathered everything I wanted, threw the duffle bag over my shoulder, and walked towards the door.

"Sorry man, you picked the wrong day to show up here," I told him as he realized he was about to be blown up in the building.

I walked out and past the truck. The kid was sitting in the front seat of the truck patiently waiting for his dad to return. I tried not to look in his direction as I walked by the truck. Though I tried not to look, the little bright-eyed kid looked up and saw me. He smiled and waved to me.

The thought of Rayna crossed my mind. He was about the same age as her when I took her dad from her. Now I love her like my own daughter, and I am going to make this little boy an orphan. I took about two more steps.

"Dammit!" I said to myself.

I put the bag down and headed back toward the vault. I knew this was going to be a bad decision and this guy would be one of the people haunting me down. But at least I know I was not going to kill him with his kid around.

I entered the vault as he was trying to free himself from the zip ties and ripped the tape from his mouth.

"Why the hell did you bring a kid here?" I frustratingly asked him, knowing I was about to break all the rules in this industry.

"I was leaving." He spoke. "I could no longer take people's lives and commit crimes in the name of justice. I had hidden some cash in here and I was coming to get it before my son, and I disappeared forever."

"You were quitting?" I asked him in shock. "Nobody quits. They would haunt you down and kill you."

"Yes, I know. But me and my boy are going to disappear, and they won't ever find us."

"I know I will probably regret this." I asserted as I cut the zip ties from his hands.

He scrambled to his feet. "Thank you and you will not regret this as you will never see me and my son again." He walked toward the communication tower. He slowly removed the explosives from the corner of the tower and opened a drawer. He pulled out a backpack and opened it, showing me a bag full of money. "I have been storing this here, planning our getaway."

"Leave now, because I am about to take this whole system down."

We both exited the vault. He jumped in the truck and pulled out of the parking lot, I picked up my duffle bag and walked to the end of the building. I turned to look at the building as I pulled out the detonator. I watched as the entire building exploded when I flipped the switch.

I had taken out Ghost Squad's entire arsenal and their communication system. I pulled my hoodie over my head then turned and walked away as the fire was bellowing from the building.

The next phase of the plan was to hit them where it really hurt, and I needed to do so before everybody caught on and they beefed up security. It was time to go after their money.

Ghost Squad used a butcher shop in the middle of downtown as a front to keep their cash. The refrigerated area didn't just store meat, it contained millions in cash seized from drug raids and used to fund the operation.

The shop was always guarded by a cashier and a butcher, both of which were Ghost Squad trainees. There would never be fewer than two people at the store, usually in the morning. Around lunchtime, more help came and there would be as many as four guys working at the store. I would have to go now before lunchtime and more people would arrive.

I arrived at the butcher shop and set up across the street to observe the shop. It was a slow morning, and I could only see one person in the shop. I would need to go quickly before any others arrived. There was one customer in the shop, and as soon as they left, I would make my move.

The one guard in the store was helping this customer carry meat to their car. I decided to sneak into the building while they were loading the vehicle. I crossed the street at the intersection and waited for them to bring out another load. I walked toward the door as they exited, and they turned in the other direction taking the meat to the vehicle.

I snuck in the door as they walked out and pressed the button unlocking the freezer. I walked past the frozen meat and to the area where the cash was stored in boxes. I opened a box, and it was empty. I opened another; it too was empty. The same for a third, nothing was there.

I knew they kept the cash here; this was strange. I shut the lid to the box. There was an empty storage container next to the boxes. I looked closer and realized those were the same containers they were just taking out of the store. Damn, I better get out of here. They were expecting me, and they moved the money.

I turned to run out of the freezer and was met by three men as I exited the freezer, all wearing hoodies and pointing guns in my direction. I had been set up. I stopped in my tracks and raised my hands in the air. One of the men reached and grabbed the backpack from me.

And everything went black.

Somebody had hit me on the head knocking me to the ground. I was lying there and could see from the reflection in the glass they were all pointing their guns at me.

"Don't move," One of them said to me.

One of them searched for me, pulling a pistol from my belt line.

"Sit him up," I heard one say as the other two grabbed me by my arms and sat me up on my knees.

"We were told to look you in your eyes and give you a message before we killed you," the bearded man with a raspy voice stated as he looked me eye to eye. He handed his gun to the man to his right and as he pulled out some gloves from his pocket.

These were the lead-filled gloves we used to force information from suspects. They were under orders to beat me before they put a bullet in my head.

"Fuck you and Command," I yelled realizing that this would likely be the man that was about to take my life.

Suddenly, both other guys fell to the floor. In shock, we both looked at them laying there and could see them bleeding from their heads. Both had been shot dead.

He suddenly turned toward the front door as I heard the door close. I could not see as he was standing in front of me blocking my view.

Abruptly, he falls face-first to the ground. I was on my knees with three dead guys around me. Then I heard the voice.

"We figured you could use the help," I heard coming from the door. I covered my eyes as the glare of the sun created a silhouette of two men. I stood up to get a better view and there stood Gerald and Rob. I could not have been happier to see them at that moment.

"How did you two find me?" I questioned them.

"Those hoodies we gave you had tracking devices sewn in them. When we asked you about coming, we knew you would say no, but we were coming anyway," Rob said.

"We could not let you go at this alone, and you all had become family to us," Gerald stated.

"Besides, looks like if we had not followed you, this morning would have gone a lot differently," Rob said.

"I am thankful that you did show up, but I have no time for a reunion. They have Rayna and I need to go and get her back," I said to break up the happy reunion.

They moved the cash, which meant they had an idea I was coming, and they are now on the defensive. I am sure they have moved Rayna again now, making things even harder. I know Rob and Gerald do not know this city, but we are going to have to split up if we ever expect to find her.

I looked around to find a piece of paper and a pen. I figured there were four or five likely places they would have her and we needed to get to each one quickly. I gave Gerald and Rob a couple of addresses each and we all went our separate ways to try and find Rayna.

I rushed over to a safe house Ghost Squad used in the area. I thought if she was not there, I could at least get some information from somebody there to help me try and locate her. I pulled up to this ordinary-looking house in the middle of a quiet community.

It looked as if there was nobody there, as I circled around the house trying to get a look. I broke the windowpane in the back door and entered the house. I carefully entered the house looking around and it was empty, but when I entered the kitchen, I could see a coffee pot on the stove. I touched it and it was still warm. Somebody was recently here.

I continued searching the house bedroom by bedroom. I entered the back bedroom. Unlike the other rooms, the bed here looked as if somebody had been sitting on it. There was a chair against the wall positioned so that it was facing the bed, like somebody that would be standing guard watching a person.

Rayna had been here. I pulled the covers back on the bed and checked the drawers and the closet for any hint. I looked under the bed. When I got up, I noticed something etched into the nightstand. I moved the nightstand to get a better look.

"Honda 4TDKY11" was sketched into the wood. It was a license plate number. The city had a very sophisticated network of cameras with license tag readers. If this was indeed something Rayna did, I could easily track down this car and her.

I ran out to the car and grabbed the laptop from the trunk. Ghost Squad used a back door to hack into the surveillance system and chances are that hole had not been closed. I rushed back to the house, opening the computer. Praying that I could access the system still using that same back door.

I was in, and they did not fix that issue. Now, I just need to find out the last known hits on this tag in the city. The computer shows the last hit near a warehouse district just outside of downtown. I never knew Ghost Squad to have any assets in that area, but that would be a perfect place for them to hide her.

Then my phone rang. It must be them calling again. I answered the phone.

"I see you have been extremely busy," the voice on the other end stated.

I did not respond, I just held the phone and listened.

"She is alive for now, any more attempts to find her or any further attacks and you will never see her again."

I still did not speak and just listened. Listened to his voice, the background, anything to give me a clue. Suddenly, he gave the phone to Rayna.

"Mr. Stew I am fine. It will all work out and I will see you soon, just bring me the new Nikes you promised," calmly she said.

"We will be in touch." the male voice said before hanging up the phone.

I felt a sense of peace hearing her voice. I know they are in the warehouse district, and I could hear a commuter train in the background. The entire district ran parallel to the rail transit and there were at least fifteen warehouses there.

I started driving toward the district and replayed the conversation in my head repeatedly. What was I missing?

Rayna said to bring her the new Nikes I promised. I replayed that conversation in my mind. I never told her I would buy her some Nikes; I mentioned I would buy her some tennis shoes.

There was an old Nike factory a block from the warehouse district. Rayna was giving me a clue as to where they were keeping her. I needed to get to the old Nike factory before they moved here again. I called Rob and told them where they were holding her and told him and Gerald to meet me there.

"Don't go in until we get there," Rob stated as I hung up the phone.

I rushed through the streets of the city and past the warehouse district. The Nike Factory sat at the end of the street. You could see everybody on the street approaching. It was an abandoned area, so they would see me coming if I drove down the street toward the factory.

I parked a few blocks away and entered the public train station. I could approach the building on the tracks, as the train tracks were hidden by the brush and could cover my approach. I ran half a mile from the train stop to the building.

There did not appear to be any cameras on this side of the building, so I climbed the fence and onto the property. The building had not been used in over a decade. It was all boarded up. As I turned the corner to the back of the building, I saw a red Honda parked in the distance.

"Honda," was written on the nightstand. She is here.

I crept along the edge of the building towards the door near the parked car. As I approached, I could tell this was the entrance they had used. I checked the car to make sure nobody was in the car and crept up the stairs to the door.

I peeked in the glass frame and could not see anybody. I checked the door handle, and the door was unlocked. Quietly I entered the building, checking my surroundings. She was somewhere in this warehouse, and I wanted to see them before they saw me.

I could hear voices in the distance, but the empty warehouse echoed making it hard to pinpoint the area of the voices. I slowly walked forward as I could hear the voices getting louder. I peeked around a corner and saw a man standing with his back to me at the other end of the hall. Another man walked out of the door, and I was in plain sight if he was looking.

I jumped to get back behind the wall.

"What was that?" I heard one of them say.

"Something was moving over there, go check it out." The second guy said.

I could hear the boots getting closer with each step he took. I took the knife from my holster. If he got here, I needed to take him out, but I needed to do it quietly. I didn't want to alert the others and put Rayna in danger.

His steps sounded as if he was no more than ten feet away and approaching. Suddenly, just in front of him, a rat ran across the floor.

"Dammit Ray, it was just a rat. When can we get the hell out of here, I hate rodents," I heard the man say as he turned around and walked back down the hall. At least two other men were inside with him. How was I going to approach them down this long hallway?

As he was walking down the hallway, he turned and walked into the bathroom. If I was going to approach him, I needed to do it now while the others were in the room, and he could not see me coming down the hall.

I rushed to the bathroom door. Before I opened it, I could hear him inside using the bathroom. I pushed the door open.

"Ray, I didn't even check to see if the damn plumbing works in here," the guy said as I entered. I walked up behind him at the urinal. He could see me in the mirror, my gray hoodie and a gun pointing at his head. He looked over where he had placed his gun on the sink.

"Don't even think about it," I said to him. "Slowly put your hands on your head."

"Can I at least zip up my pants?" He asked.

"Slowly lower your left hand and zip your pants, don't try anything."

"You know I am trained to shoot with both hands."

"It wouldn't matter, I am trained not to miss. So, you would die here if you tried."

He zipped his pants, and I made him get on his knees. I then zip-tied his hands behind his back. I tied his feet together and then tied him to the cast iron pipe in the corner of the room.

"You know the reason you are not dying today; I know you. I know you are not a bad person, just somebody that is doing a job. I know you have got a wife and kids, so I am going to let you live. Don't make me regret it." I told him as I stuffed his mouth shut.

I knew those zip ties would not hold him long. But, by the time he broke free from them, we would be long gone.

I rushed out of the bathroom and to the door where they were holding Rayna. I looked inside and could see her there with two men. There was no quiet way to enter the room this time. I gathered myself, took a deep breath, and kicked in the door.

I quickly fired two shots killing the guy that was closest to me. I turned to the other guy. He had grabbed Rayna to use her as a shield.

"Don't try anything, or I will blow her brains out," He said, holding the gun to her head.

"Drop your gun and walk over there." He instructed me while pointing towards the wall. I slowly put my gun down and walked toward the wall. We passed each other as he was headed towards the door with Rayna still serving as his human shield. My back was against the wall as he got near the door.

He reached down and pulled a device out of a box. With one hand he turned it on and set it down. I could see it had a timer on it. He was about to blow up the room.

"She and I are walking out of here. If you come out of this door before we make the end of the hall, I will kill her." He said as he continued backing towards the door.

Next thing I heard a glass crack and he fell to the floor with Rayna. I looked out of the shattered glass in the door and saw Rob at the end of the hall with a sniper rifle. I rushed over to Rayna to see if she had been hit. I pulled the guy off her.

"Mr. Stew, did you bring the Nikes?" she quipped, making me smile as she got up off the ground.

I grabbed the incendiary device and disconnected the timing mechanism. Rob and Gerald walked through the door.

"I am not sure what you would do without us," Gerald said.

I hugged Rayna, and we all walked out the door. We walked by the bathroom as the door was still open. Rob asked, "What are you going to do about him?"

I looked in the bathroom.

"Nothing. Let's go. We came here to get Baby Girl. We got Rayna, and that's what I wanted." I said as we walked down the hall and out of the building.

CHAPTER 13

DAD

I hugged Rayna as we walked out of the building and across the parking lot. Rob and Gerald parked their car just outside of the fence beyond the parking lot.

"Are you still going to get me those Nikes?" Rayna asked, and I just smiled at her.

I looked back at the building, wondering if he had made it out. The building would blow up at any moment and he had plenty of time to free himself of those zip ties. As I turned to continue walking toward the car, I saw him out of the corner of my eye, running toward the railroad tracks.

I was relieved he had freed himself. As we reached the car, we heard a huge explosion behind us. We all turned and looked. We could see the building had blown up and was in flames. We looked at one another and got in the car. We needed to exit before the fire department got here.

As we turned off the dirt road leading away from the warehouse, we passed a gray car parked on the road. It seems I had seen that car multiple times. Nobody was in the car, maybe I was mistaken. They drove Rayna and me back to the train station to get my car.

"You guys going to come over later. We can put some food on the grill?" I asked Rob and Gerald.

"We would never turn down a meal," Gerald responded.

"Good, come by the house about 8 tonight. I guess you don't need the address." I joked, reminding them of the GPS tracker they placed in my hoodies.

I figured I could not continue to hide the truth from Rayna about her dad. It has been eating at my conscious. She probably will find out one day. I rather she hears it from me.

"Rayna let's go to the park and get a burger. We can just hang out there for a while." I told her.

It was a beautiful day out and the park was crowded. We went to the burger stand and ordered the biggest and sloppiest hamburger on earth with a milkshake to wash it down. As we waited for our food, I got up the courage to talk to Rayna about her dad.

"Rayna, I need to talk to you about something. Something I have wanted to tell you for some time." I cautiously stated. "I want to talk about your dad," I said to her as I watched to gauge her reaction.

"I really don't want to talk about that," Rayna responded.

"Stewart," we heard the man from the burger stand yell out.

"I'll get the burgers," Rayna stated and jumped up to go get our food.

I took my food, and we walked across the parking lot to find a spot in the park to sit and eat.

"Mr. Stew, you see that gray car over there? I have seen that car a lot," Rayna stated as she nodded in the direction of the car.

I turned to see if it looked like the same gray car that was near the warehouse. This is more than a coincidence. Who could be following us? I wanted to find us a place to sit and eat where I could have a good view of the park and that car.

We got a table on the pavilion that was elevated; giving me a better view of everybody in the park and that car. I could not see anybody in the car, but whoever drove it was in the crowd now.

I scanned the park looking for whoever the driver could be. Very few people are going to be out here alone; so, that person is likely alone and should be easy to spot. I could see a few people who were in the park alone.

There was a young man wearing a green shirt. But he was wearing headphones, not paying attention to anything around him.

There was a lady near the parking lot. She had a notepad. She was about five feet tall and weighed maybe one hundred pounds. She had on some cutoff jean shorts and fluorescent yellow tennis shoes. She could not be the one following us. She would not be a threat and would not be wearing those fluorescent shoes.

There was another guy who was older, and seemed like he was out of place. He just stood there looking over people at the park. He looked in my direction and we briefly locked eyes before he looked off. He didn't look like he was dressed to come sit in the park.

I ate my burger as I kept an eye on him. He stood there by himself, looking over the park and occasionally at his phone. He got a call and answered his phone. Then he started walking with a purpose. I better go and follow him to see what he was doing; this is probably the guy who has been following me.

I put my burger down and told Rayna I would be right back. He was walking towards the bathrooms. It would be ideal for me to corner him in a bathroom and not in public. I sped up to try and catch him.

He looked back as he was walking, and we locked eyes again. He turned his head and kept walking. He walked to the public bathroom and stood outside of the door. I decided to walk past him and go around the other side of the building. I was going to have to snatch him into the bathroom. I snuck around the building and peeked in the window to see if anybody was in the men's bathroom. There was nobody there.

I walked to the corner of the building; he was still standing there. I looked around and it did not look like anybody was walking toward the building or paying any attention. I better do it now.

I stepped around the corner, reached and grabbed his shoulder. Just as I touched his shoulder.

"Hey, baby." A lady said as she greeted him with a hug while walking out of the bathroom. He turned to look at me.

"I am sorry. I thought you were somebody else." I quickly said to him.

"What took you so long in the bathroom?" he asked his female friend.

"My phone died and I was using the charger to get some power. That's why I didn't see your text. But I knew you were here. I saw your truck and parked next to you." She responded.

This was obviously not the person I was looking for in the gray car. I decided to go into the bathroom since I was there.

I exited the bathroom and bumped into a lady. I knocked something out of her hand.

"I am sorry ma'am," I said as I reached down to pick up her notepad. I grabbed it and saw those fluorescent tennis shoes. It is her; she is following me.

I grabbed the notepad and handed it to her as I looked around. As she reached for the notepad, I grabbed her arm and snatched her into the bathroom. She tried to scream. I put my hand over her mouth and pushed her against the door.

"Why the hell are you following me?" I said as I had one hand over her mouth and another around her neck. I lifted her off the ground by her neck, her fluorescent shoes barely touched the ground.

"Command sent you?" I asked as I was about to strangle her to death in the bathroom.

"Answer me dammit!" I said irately. I could see tears forming in her eyes and she was gasping for air.

I lowered her back to the ground, taking my hand from around her neck, giving her a chance to breathe and answer. She gasped for air and mumbled something. I removed my hand from her mouth, so she could talk.

"I am a reporter with Citywide News," she said as she gathered her breath.

"Bullshit!" I spoke.

"I am. Check my bag. My work badge is in there."

I reached into her bag and saw her ID, 'Susan Chambers – Investigative reporter'.

"Why are you following me?" I asked her, curious as to how much she had seen.

She went on to tell me that she has been doing a story on Ghost Squad for about six months. She told me an anonymous source inside the unit tipped her about investigating it. She had not heard from the source since that time, but he told her enough to get an investigation started.

She told me she was ready to release the story. She has seen many of the members disappear or found dead. She then told me that Command was simply a puppet, taking orders from the Mayor with no real power.

"I heard you were back. I wanted to talk to you before I published the article," she stated.

"Good luck with your article, but I won't be a part of it," I said as I let her go and walked out the door.

She ran out behind me. "Don't you want to know who tried to kill you? Don't you want to know who could be coming after you next? Don't you want to end this forever so you and that little girl can live in peace?"

I listened as I walked away. I stopped when she mentioned Rayna. I turned to her.

"You can help me end it all."

I told her I was having a cookout at my house. I gave her my number and told her to call me. I would tell her where to meet me later. We would pick her up and take her to the house. I could not give her the address because I didn't know who could be following her. I know if she was with me, I could make sure there was not a tail.

I made it back to the pavilion and Rayna had finished eating.

"Who was that lady? I thought you were going to kill her when you pulled her into the bathroom," Rayna said to me, rather nonchalantly.

I just looked at her. She seemed to have become too comfortable with violence and this lifestyle. I was shocked she saw me, but even more shocked she did not seem disturbed by it at all.

Later that evening, Susan called. Rayna and I went out to meet her and brought her to the house. We were all there eating and enjoying ourselves. Susan and I went out to the backyard to give her a chance to ask me whatever she needed to know.

I told her everything I knew. She told me many things about Ghost Squad I did not know and confirmed many other things I had believed to be true. She stated that she was turning in the article to her editor in the morning, and it would probably run on the website that evening.

She showed proof which tied the squad to the Mayor. She also showed that he greenlighted the squad to help boost his ratings to win an election. The Mayor then used the squad as his personal muscle to not only artificially reduce crime rates, but to help him continue to cover up a pay-for-play scheme he had with contractors in the city to get city contracts.

She told me she was following Ghost Squad the day they attacked me at my house, when they shot me and left me for dead. She had pictures of them at Stephanie's house minutes before they blew up her home while we were in Barbados.

She had the name of every officer who had worked for Ghost Squad. She detailed each one who no longer worked there. Whether they were killed in the line of duty, assassinated for asking too many questions, disappeared, or have not been heard from, she had information on them all.

I was in awe listening to her.

"Stewart, I still haven't told you half of the information I have. It's just that much," Susan said. "But I am not the first one who started asking questions about this 'Ghost Squad.' The other reporter mysteriously died in a car accident before he ever released the story. That is why I back up this story every day and hide a copy. Daily I back it up and keep a copy at my house. But each week I put a copy in a storage unit downtown."

We wrapped up the evening before taking her back to her car. Rayna and I dropped her off. She stated she was going to go into the store to grab some candy and would call me later if she had any more questions. Rayna and I drove off as she walked into the store.

Stephanie, Rayna, and I were just watching TV as a breaking news story scrolled across the screen.

"Vehicle explosion at Ponce Market kills one and injures a dozen. Details on the 11 o'clock news."

Rayna and I looked at each other. We dropped Susan off at Ponce Market. They cut into the news teaser, and you could see the charred remains of what looked like the same car Susan had been driving. Later, the news came on and confirmed, "Susan Chamber of Citywide News was killed in an automobile explosion. Sources state there was a gas can in her back seat that accidentally ignited, causing the vehicle to burst into flames."

I just sat there in silence. Didn't want to speak about it and scare Rayna and Stephanie. They had seen and experienced enough violence.

"What are you going to do about it, Mr. Stew?" Rayna asked me. I was shocked she had asked that question. The look on her face was one that insisted I do something.

The news came back on, and we watched in silence. I was thinking to myself about what Susan said, and the possibility of being able to have Rayna, Stephanie and I to live in peace. Now that she told me where the buck stopped. I could go after the head of Ghost Squad and end it forever.

I was glad she told me where to find backup copies of her story. I needed to make sure I got those copies to get her story out to everybody. I wanted to make sure she was not killed for nothing. Something good was going to come from her work. It would not be in vain.

I needed to get to her storage unit and house to get the electronic backup before anybody else thought about finding them.

The next morning, I woke up and set out to get those backup copies. The storage unit was on the way to the house, so it was the first stop. She had a small storage room and she said it would be just a few boxes in there.

I went up to the third floor and looked around to find her unit. Unit 333. I found the unit and noticed the lock on the unit was missing. I opened the door to the storage unit. There was nothing inside. I looked around to ensure I was at the right storage unit. I was, however, somebody had beat me to it.

I needed to rush to the house. I am sure if they knew about the storage unit, they might go to the house. I pulled up in the driveway of her house. When I walked up to her door, I could see the door had been kicked in. I pulled out my gun and pushed the door open.

I saw the house had been ransacked, as it looked like they had already been there looking for other copies. I saw the refrigerator had been left open and a gallon of milk was sitting on the counter. My first thought was they found the jump drive.

I rushed over to grab the milk. I poured the milk out into the sink, and there it was. She had a sealed jump drive in the milk. They did not find it. I rushed out of the house and went to the nearest print shop to open the drive to see what was on it.

I went through the documents on the computer. Lots more information in this file that Susan hadn't told me. She never mentioned the interview she had with a former officer in Ghost Squad which connected the Mayor to the assassination of his political opponent, and how they made it look like a heart attack. The notes from his interview detail his order from the Mayor to carry out the assassination and how.

They injected him with aconite, one of the deadliest poisons on earth which is virtually untraceable. Aconite poison looks like heart failure, so it was easy to pass off as a heart attack. I had seen enough and shut the computer down to head out to find the Mayor.

Today was the day for the monthly City Council meeting, so you knew the Mayor would be there at the beginning of the meeting. I rushed down to City Hall and waited outside of the council chambers. After a few minutes, the Mayor walked out with his security.

"Mayor Ingram, we need to talk," I said as I approached him. His security cut me off before I could get too close.

"Don't touch me!" I said, knocking the security detail's hands off me.

"I know who you are. We don't need to talk. As a matter of fact, I should probably have you arrested," he stated.

I was shocked he recognized me, and I reached into my pocket. His security pulled their guns when they saw me reach in my pocket.

"Whoa, I am just getting my phone," I said to them with one hand in the air moving deliberately as not to make any sudden movements.

I pulled out my phone, showing it to them. I hit the send button.

I heard a phone buzz.

"Mayor Ingram, you just got a message from me. You should look at it, and as I said, we need to talk." I insisted.

He pulled out his phone and opened the email. You could see the look of shock on his face as he opened it. He started scrolling through his phone. He looked up from his phone and you could see the nervous energy as his hand started to tremor.

"Come to my office," he said.

I looked at his security.

"Can you two put those up now." I said asking them to lower their guns.

We all walked towards the Mayor's office. You could see how visibly shaken the Mayor was. We walked into his office, and I took a seat. He told his security detail to give us a minute alone. I turned and watched them walk out of the room.

I explained to him everything in the email. The email had copies of bank accounts showing deposits from his bid rigging of city contracts. The email had details about various murders, including that of his political rival. It had an interview with a former 'Command' of Ghost Squad and him detailing the dynamics of Ghost Squad. There was enough in the email to send the Mayor to jail for the rest of his life.

"What do you want?" he asked. "You want money? I can arrange to get you however much you want." the Mayor stated as his voice started to crack.

"I don't want money. I want my freedom and peace of mind," I said.

"That is easy. I can give you all of that," the Mayor said, sounding relieved.

"It is not that easy," I said to him. "Part of my peace of mind is taking down everybody who turned Ghost Squad rogue, and making them pay for it," I said as his expression turned to worry again.

I got up from my chair and walked toward the door.

As I got to the door I turned to him. "I got peace of mind now. When I sent you that email, it also went to every newspaper and TV station in the city. I just wanted to have you see my face when I sent it so you knew who did it to you." I said to him as I turned and walked out the door.

He picked up his phone and frantically scrolled through it trying to verify what I said. As he picked up his phone, an email came through.

"Damn!!!" is all the email said. It was from the editor at Citywide News. He was replying to the email I had blasted out. The Mayor now had confirmation that the whole world would soon know about his dirty dealings.

The Mayor had no intentions of facing the press on this and knew he would be spending the rest of his life in jail. He decided there was another way out. As I reached the bottom floor to exit City Hall. You could hear a gunshot ring out through the atrium and echo throughout the building.

The Mayor had decided to take another way out. I kept walking as I had no sympathy for him.

I got in the car and headed home. Home to be with my new family before I closed the last chapter to this rogue unit of Ghost Squad. And that was making sure 'Command' was punished for his part.

I arrived back at the house to see Rayna and Stephanie on the porch relaxing. It was a pleasant sight to see, and that made me smile. As I approached the porch, Stephanie said, "We saw the news report about the Mayor."

I just nodded my head and sat down.

"Mr. Stew, I think I want to talk about my daddy now," Rayna said, catching me off guard.

Stephanie stood up. "I think I will let you two talk in private," she said as she walked back into the house.

Rayna was a very perceptive person. I would have to give her all of the details of what I did for a living, and how it all tied to her dad. I explained to her that I once worked for Ghost Squad, the same people who have been after us.

I told Rayna how the squad started with good intentions, and how greed and power corrupted it. I explained to her what happened to the Mayor and everything Susan had found. She listened intently and patiently.

"How does all of this tie to my dad?" she abruptly interrupted.

I took a deep breath and looked at her. I knew I had to tell her, and there was no easy way to say it.

"Rayna, your dad was into some really bad things, and had crossed the wrong people." I started explaining to her.

She knew her dad was into some bad things, so none of this was news to her.

"Command ordered for your dad to be killed," I told her.

"So, it was Command who wanted my dad dead?" she repeated to me.

I just nodded, waiting for her response and the chance to tell her the other part of the story.

"But there is something else I must tell you," I paused and grabbed her hand. "I was the one they sent after your dad."

There was an awkward silence. She didn't say anything. I looked at her, waiting for a response. Then she pulled her hand away from me. My heart dropped. I felt at that moment I had lost her.

She stood up and walked away.

"Rayna?"

She did not respond nor acknowledge me as she walked off the porch and down the sidewalk. I figured I should give her some space. I don't know. I don't have any kids and have no idea how to deal with teenage girls. But this moment was one nobody would be prepared to deal with.

I went into the house and told Stephanie I had broken the news to Rayna, and she walked away.

"Give her a few minutes and then go talk to her. She usually goes to the benches down by the lake," Stephanie told me.

"I am scared. You didn't see her face. I think I lost her with this," I said to Stephanie.

She walked up and gave me a hug, understanding that I was really shaken by the thoughts of losing Rayna.

"It is going to be fine, baby," Stephanie said to me.

We sat there and agreed to give her about thirty minutes before I went to go and find her. I was nervous as my mind raced. Wondering what she was thinking, what she might do or say. I needed to go and find Rayna. I left the house to head to the lake to talk to her.

I got to the lake and did not see her near the benches. I looked around the area and did not see her. I saw a gum wrapper near the bench. That was the gum she always chewed, so I knew she had been here. I called back to the house asking Stephanie if Rayna had come home. She had not.

I knew of a few other places she could be. I walked all over the neighborhood and could not find her. I was worried, but I was sure she would return home. I decided to go back home to wait for her. I was about two miles from the house.

I got an alert from my phone. I pulled out my phone and it was the security system. Command was at the house and had kicked the front door in. Stephanie was there alone. I called Stephanie. She answered the phone with it on speaker.

"Command is in the house," I yelled into the phone as I sprinted home.

I could hear Stephanie scream as the phone disconnected. I had to get home quickly as he was here to kill everybody. This was not going to be a kidnapping.

I sprinted the two miles, thinking about what I may find when I got home. As I approached the house, I heard a gunshot. It stopped me in my tracks. Breathing heavily from the long run. Sweating profusely and nervous. I was too late.

I rushed to the door, fearing the worst. I did not see anything in the front room. She answered the phone in the kitchen. I walked toward the kitchen. I paused before entering. I turned into the kitchen with my gun drawn.

I saw a lifeless body on the floor. I saw a person standing over the body, wearing a gray hoodie pulled over their head. I was too late. Ghost Squad had killed Stephanie.

A person standing near the refrigerator caught my attention. It was Stephanie standing there. I looked back at the body on the floor, and then the person standing over the body in the gray hoodie. They turned towards me looking down. I could not see the face.

I saw the gun in their hand as they turned. They looked up and pulled the hoodie off their head.

It was Rayna.

"You said Command called for my dad to be killed. Now we are even. I got revenge for his death," Rayna somberly said.

I walked over and took the gun from her before embracing her.

"I don't like calling you Mr. Stew. Can I call you Dad?" Rayna asked as I hugged her. I smiled. I was happy and at peace. We were all safe now.